The Staff

The Staff

Divine power in the wrong hands

Jay Pintado

STRATEGIQ

A catalogue record for this
book is available from the
National Library of Australia

ISBN: 978-0-6488012-0-7 (Paperback)
ISBN 978-0-6488012-1-4 (Hardback)
ISBN: 978-0-6488012-2-1 (Ebook)

Publisher: StrategIQ

Editing – Eddie Albrecht, Pickawoowoo Publishing Group
Cover Cube Concept: Patricia Pintado
Cover Creation and Artwork—Laila Savolainen, Pickawoowoo
Publishing Group
Interior Design—Pickawoowoo Publishing Group

Printed & Channel Distribution: Lightning Source | Ingram (USA/
UK/EUROPE/AUS)

Table of Contents

1

Gaza Strip 1967

In a small war-torn town in the Gaza Strip, the afternoon sun shines on the turret of an Israeli Army tank as it slowly climbs over a mound of debris. The surrounding earth rumbles, releasing a heavy dust which engulfs the air. The sight of the tank causes a small group of civilians to scatter, hiding in what little structures there are left in the town. The tank is part of a regular patrol covering approximately 360 square kilometres of land which forms the Gaza Strip. The tank is flanked by six Israeli soldiers, crouched and skulking three along each side of the tank. The soldiers come to what's left of a building and immediately encounter a rock-throwing group of youths. They are no match for the tank. The massive armoured beast slows then comes to a complete halt to protect its six anxious soldiers who take a knee as they cautiously study the actions of their enemy. The civilians far outnumber the soldiers and scamper into a ruined building and begin to rummage through the surrounding debris for weapons, sticks, stones, hard plastics, anything they can throw. Despite the fact it is densely populated, the Gaza Strip is not recognised as part of any extant country, it has no label or identity. The surrounding population of mixed religion battle for ownership.

A civilian pauses, noticing what appears to be a black pipe protruding out of tangled reinforced concrete. He tries to pull it out but it won't budge. He tries several times but the black pipe does not move. With the tank turret now noisily pivoting to take aim at the ruined building and the soldiers preparing to engage, the civilian places his foot where the pipe leaves the concrete and makes several attempts to bend the pipe upward then downward and right to left. On his third attempt the pipe finally snaps in half. The civilian holds the pipe up admiring it like a knight would his sword. It's not like anything he has seen before. He then slowly waves it and slaps it against his hand a few times, it has some weight to it and it's hard and very strong, it's perfect, he smirks, he's armed. It's the best weapon he has ever had in all his skirmishes with the Israelis. He cautiously hides behind a crumbling archway and assesses the distance between the tank and the soldiers.

"Brace!" shouts Shapiro, the most experienced though still young Israeli soldier as he holds his headset and follows the tank commander's orders.

The other soldiers prepare themselves as the tank takes aim. Immediately the civilians launch a volley of rocks and sticks at Shapiro as well as Green and

Goldberg, his fellow soldiers who are crouched down next to him along the left side of the tank. Shapiro is hit with minor rubble and brushes it off before slowly standing peering above the front left corner of the tank to assess the enemy. The civilian at the crumbling archway seizes the opportunity and steps out hurling the black pipe like a spinning tomahawk. The end strikes Shapiro's cheek bone hard and he drops on all fours. The tank instantly redirects its turret in the direction of the crumbling archway and returns fire with rapid bursts from its machine guns. The civilians are forced to scramble taking cover in what's left of the town's other buildings. Goldberg, a young and relatively new soldier to Gaza, was next to Shapiro the entire time. He grabs Shapiro by the back of the vest and drags him up forcing him to sit upright against the wheels of the stationary tank. Noticing his fellow soldiers are down, Green, the third soldier along the left side, grabs Shapiro's headset and moves to the front left corner of the tank. Green tells the tank commander to keep the tank stationary as he takes a knee and begins to examine the extent of the injuries to Shapiro.

The tank commander takes advantage of the break in combat and emerges from the tank turret to observe his fallen soldier. The civilians take the opportunity and slither from their crevasses to rearm themselves with debris. The Israeli tank commander immediately notices the enemy has reassembled to advance and seizes his turret machine gun sending sporadic bursts of gunfire towards the civilians to provide protection for the downed soldiers. Green and Goldberg stand to return fire leaving a shaken Shapiro on the ground leaning against the tank. The two soldiers move to the front left corner and kneel as they aim their weapons. The civilians again scramble into the ruins.

The tank commander barks orders and the tank turret moves to take aim at another damaged building where most of the enemy have taken cover. The tank commander has the dissidents on the run.

Shapiro is still seated on the ground resting against the tank. He repeatedly tries to clear his vision by blinking and wiping his eyes. Still in a daze, he scans the rocks and sticks around him to find what knocked him to the ground. One piece of debris stands out, a black pipe. He picks it up and runs his fingers along its length cleaning off dust which barely moves. This pipe is different, it's not a pipe, not metal at all. It's smooth and feels more like petrified wood the length of a cane. Shapiro notices a glint and is drawn to a small orange object imbedded in a knot in the timber. He comes to the knot and notices the object is as smooth as glass. Shapiro licks his fingers and gently rubs the glass to clean it but the dirt is stubborn. He tries again licking his thumb rubbing hard on the orange glass to clean it. In an instant silence falls around the battlefield. The screaming of men and the barking of orders cease. The tank engine continues.

Goldberg immediately notices his fellow soldier Green, who was right next to him, on the ground motionless. He looks up and sees the enemy that failed to hide in the ruins lying still in the rubble. Goldberg then looks up to see the tank commander slumped over the turret opening, he is dead. They're all dead.

Goldberg then looks down over his shoulder, still trying to clear his vision and with his stick in hand, he notices Shapiro staring straight back at him. Goldberg scouts the battlefield one more time, there is no movement anywhere. He shoulders his weapon and kneels next to Shapiro.

"What the hell happened?" he asks Shapiro, puzzled and concerned.

Shapiro tightly grasps the black stick to his chest as he looks up and responds quickly shaking his head and shrugging his shoulders.

"I don't know. I...I..." Shapiro stammers nervously.

Goldberg moves to the back of the tank and notices the other three soldiers along the right-hand side of the tank, lying in the rubble. They are not moving. He looks at the battlefield again and returns his attention to Shapiro, frowning as he stares down at him and the black object in Shapiro's hand. Shapiro slowly raises the pipe to his face for a closer look, his entire face focused on the smooth object.

"All I did was pick up this stick and clean the orange glass," he struggles to tell Goldberg between gasps of air.

Both men are scared and confused and can't stop staring at the black object. Goldberg hammers the butt of his weapon against the tank to see if anyone inside is alive. The tank driver responds with hammering of his own. Goldberg grabs the headset off Green as two of the crew emerge from the tank.

"Help me get these men on the tank," Goldberg barks, ordering the tank crew to pick up the fallen soldiers and load them onto the tank so they can all return to base. As the tank crew scurries Shapiro rests against the turret and closes his eyes.

It's present day in a dimly lit room of a New York hospital. An old and weak Shapiro is lying motionless with a full head bandage, the result of a fall at his home. Multiple tubes protrude from the old man's nose, neck, arms and torso.

"Grandpa. Grandpa are you okay?" whispers Hershel Rosen, Shapiro's grandson who is sitting beside the bed holding his grandfather's hand.

Hershel has just listened to Shapiro's amazing story of his battle in the Gaza Strip. Shapiro opens his teary eyes. They are as wide-eyed as that day in Gaza. In a weak crackling voice, he looks at Hershel.

"And that's what happened. My attic, green army locker, find it, promise me, promise me you will take it to the old rabbi, tell no one."

Shapiro barely manages to get the words out between struggling deep breaths.

"Okay I will, I will. You just rest now," Hershel promises softly in an attempt to calm his grandfather.

Shapiro squeezes Hershel's hand as if to acknowledge the promise. The room is quiet – not even the street sounds of New York can be heard. The two men are still and stare at each other. Before long Shapiro smiles at Hershel and closes his eyes. Only a moment passes before Shapiro loosens his grip on Hershel's hand, he takes his last breath before quietly and peacefully passing away.

2

Present day

A cold wind and driving rain buffet a simple old timber house nestled under a giant oak tree in Syracuse, New York. Hershel's mother, Shapiro's only daughter, and her husband moved into the house owned by Shapiro and cared for him in his final years. Hershel and his parents reflect on the day's events, remembering and honouring Shapiro and saying their final goodbyes as they laid him to rest.

Hershel wanders through the old home and reminisces. Memories flood back to a time when he was a child visiting the home often and playing with his grandfather's old toys. He comes to the sitting room where his mother and father are gazing blankly at the television. Hershel stays standing next to them and watches too. He takes a deep breath to prepare to ask a question in an effort to ease the tension but before he utters a single word, and with eyes transfixed on the television, his mother, in some sort of telepathic way, waves her hand down gesturing for Hershel to be quiet. Hershel concentrates on the television as his father scrambles for the remote control to turn up the volume.

Tonight's leading news story excitedly claims that the world is on the cusp of one of its most important milestones in the struggle for peace as the United Nations is on the verge of establishing a new Council for Religious Coexistence. It's a giant leap forward in a world incessantly consumed with religious conflict. The news provides details that the first crucial step in forming the new council has been completed as countries have acknowledged the major religions that will have a seat and represent their faiths. Hershel is semi-interested. He has heard enough and leaves the room.

As he enters the downstairs guest room Hershel takes off his jacket and one of his grandfather's ties he wore to the funeral. He places his backpack on a small old desk. He unzips the bag and takes out an unwashed t-shirt and track pants to get comfortable. Shapiro's funeral was particularly difficult for Hershel's mother. In the coming days Hershel knows he will need to provide support and help his mother where he can. She has already mentioned the need to go through Shapiro's belongings but that exercise will result in more grief than Hershel's mother can bear right now.

At dinner that night there is little conversation. Hershel is in two minds about bringing up his grandfather's story about Gaza despite the fact his mind is consumed by the black stick with the orange glass in the knot. He can't contain himself any longer and decides to say something. Easing into his question he asks his mother cautiously, "Mum, did grandpa ever talk about his time with the Israeli Army?"

Hershel's mother shakes her head and hesitates. "Your grandfather never really liked talking about it," she answers, all the while never looking up and making eye contact with her son.

Hershel doesn't push the issue, it's not the time. No more questions tonight. As dinner ends the Rosens tidy up in silence before everyone retires to their rooms.

In the guest room Hershel sits on the bed and scans the surroundings. He notices many items on the bookshelf, mainly old toys that bring back memories of playing with his grandfather. The day's events have caught up with Hershel and he begins to shed a tear before composing himself. He stands and makes his way towards a dresser where an old stainless-steel jet aircraft is displayed. There are ceramic Napoleonic War soldiers on the shelf which Hershel holds and closely studies – he remembers playing with them and it brings a smile to his face. He returns to the bed where he lays down, hands behind his head, staring at the ceiling. Shapiro's Gaza tale again invades his thoughts. Wide awake he makes several attempts to forget the story.

Hershel is in his third year of a political science degree. The first two years were a breeze but he is now finding it difficult resulting in the need to move into an apartment in the city to be closer to the college and library. Tonight, he is restless. He gets out of bed and walks to the desk. He moves his backpack from the desk to the chair and removes his laptop and books in the hope of doing some study. He stops, moves his bag back down to the floor and sits on the chair with his elbows on the desk as his hands cradle his head. He drops his shoulders and sighs. He can't concentrate and can't forget the promise he made to his grandfather.

The next morning, with little sleep but ample contemplation, Hershel gives in to his curiosity and decides to explore the attic. He will look for the old green army locker Shapiro mentioned on his hospital bed. He can hear his parents having breakfast, a meal that's not really part of Hershel's regime. After washing his face and still wearing his track pants and old t-shirt, he arms himself with a small flashlight and makes his way to the hallway on the second floor. Immediately he notices the pull-down string that releases a loft ladder which leads to the attic space. He gently pulls the string but finds it difficult to dislodge from the ceiling. He pauses and takes a deep breath and with a little more effort it comes loose and finds the floor. Dust, the volume of which equals the discovery of a pharaoh's tomb, hits Hershel in the face forcing him backwards. Herschel composes himself and removes a handkerchief from his pocket. He folds it into a triangle and covers his mouth, tying the ends behind his head. He looks in the hallway mirror and shakes his head free from dust. With a handkerchief mask and a face full of dust he has taken on the appearance of a wild west bank robber. He begins to slowly climb the loft ladder into the attic. The noise interrupts his parents' breakfast. They stop eating and close their eyes before holding hands as they begin to pray in Hebrew believing the noise above is Shapiro's ghost.

Hershel enters the dark attic. The thick layer of dust and creaking floorboards evidence that no one has accessed this space for some time. Hershel continues further as a stale and musky smell takes over the air. He turns on his small flashlight and begins to scan the room hoping to locate the old green army locker. The only other source of light is emanating from the open loft ladder, and Hershel's flashlight is playing up, on for a while then off, then on again. He looks for a light switch but finds nothing. Hershel tolerates the intermittent light and follows it as it feebly reveals small areas of the room. There is an old small desk near the loft ladder opening and his quick scan doesn't easily locate a locker. In an opposite corner he decides to move a pile of boxes and bags of old clothes but there is nothing underneath. In another corner a small chest of drawers, again nothing. But in the furthest corner he sees it, an old rusty locker with barely any remnants of army green paint. Hershel walks over and drags the metal crate across the attic floor before placing it next to the old desk to make the most of the light from the open loft ladder.

Back downstairs, Hershel's parents are clearing and cleaning up after breakfast. The noise created by Hershel dragging the old metal locker across the attic floor makes them drop plates and cutlery and sends chills up their spines. As Hershel's father stays still and continues to listen, Hershel's mother begins to pray in Hebrew for Shapiro's ghost to pass over into the afterlife.

"Sorry about the noise," Hershel yells down from the attic.

His loud voice makes his parents jump again before they realise it's Hershel and shake their heads.

Back in the attic Hershel discovers a rusty padlock on the locker. He busily goes through the desk drawer in search of a key. He finds a letter opener and a spoon before finally finding a screwdriver deciding to use it on the padlock. He kneels on the floor next to the locker and inserts the screwdriver into the rusted lock, it's been closed for some time but it is weak. He twists the screwdriver and with little effort the lock snaps off. Hershel lays the flashlight on top of the desk to provide some light as he squats down to carefully open the lid of the locker. He handles the lid delicately and as the locker opens an Israeli Army uniform and helmet appear, neatly folded and as crisp as the day they were stored by his grandfather. Hershel takes a deep breath and removes the items gently. Casting his eyes over them he smirks and nods before placing them on the desk. He knows he's close to his treasure.

He now has access to the next layer. Papers and folders cover the entire length of the locker which Hershel gathers quickly and places in a pile on the floor, not bothering to review their contents. The next items must date back to Shapiro's younger days, especially his Bar Mitzvah, a 13-year-old Jewish boy's coming of age celebration. He finds old cards of congratulation, a small cap – the *kippa* or *yarmulke* – a scarf and a prayer shawl or *tallit*. They are in fragile condition but still intact. Hershel carefully removes the religious materials placing them on the inside of the locker lid. There is another *tallit* lying in the next layer. This *tallit* is more elaborate, more modern and certainly in better condition. It is sitting neatly laid out nestled between two old fashioned umbrellas and just as long. It appears to be wrapped around something.

As Hershel removes the two umbrellas as the sound of heavy rain begins to fall on the attic roof. He delicately lifts the *tallit* and it's stiff as a board; there is something inside, perhaps a third umbrella Hershel thinks to himself. He slowly gets to his feet and carefully places the *tallit* on the small old desk. It is heavier than any umbrella.

Hershel steps back and begins to pace nervously alongside the small old desk. His mouth is dry as he pulls down the handkerchief from his face. Could it be that simple? he asks himself. Hershel picks up the flashlight and inserts the handle into his mouth to ensure he has ample light and both hands free to unwrap the *tallit*.

Unsure of where to begin he nervously and hesitatingly pulls back one end of the cloth.

"Hershel are you okay up there?" his mother yells at the top of her voice from the bottom of the loft ladder breaking the nervous silence.

Hershel jumps forcing him to spit out his small flashlight as it hit the back of his throat almost swallowing it.

"Yes, yes I'm okay, be down in a minute," his shaky voice belts back.

His mother's timing couldn't have been worse, now Hershel's heart is beating twice as fast. He picks up the flashlight and bangs it into his hand a few times until it provides consistent and adequate light. He takes a deep breath, places the flashlight back into his mouth and returns to the old desk and continues to lift off the *tallit*. With a little shake the *tallit* reveals a black stick greeted by a loud clap of thunder which scares Hershel and draws his attention upward to the ceiling. He gazes back down and shines his flashlight directly on the object. It's just as his grandfather described.

As Hershel removes the *tallit* entirely, the entire stick is revealed and he notices the orange glass in the knot. He quickly covers everything up and pushes himself away from the small old desk. Again, Hershel paces nervously and even faster this time across the length of the attic tripping over a box or two trying to summon up the courage to pick up and hold the object. A thousand thoughts run through his mind especially his promise to his grandfather. He is in the thick of it now. He pulls out a chair and sits at the desk and composes himself. Slowly and gently Hershel picks up the object admiring its age, its colour and smell. He holds the black stick up raising it closer to his face. The moment is interrupted by another louder clap of thunder. Hershel jumps again and rolls his eyes sick of getting scared. He looks at the stick again but is frustrated by the lack of light which prevents him having a close look. By now Hershel is a bundle of nerves; the darkness, the dust, the thunder, his mother's yelling and finding the black stick sees him edgy and tense. He quickly wraps the object back into the *tallit* and returns to the locker packing away all the other items except the *tallit* as he closes the lid. He walks quickly on tiptoes to the open loft ladder and begins to make his way down with *tallit* in hand.

As he reaches halfway, he changes his grip on the *tallit* and he continues down the ladder before reaching the floor. Hershel takes a deep breath as if to give thanks the ordeal is over. He looks at the *tallit* and celebrates his discovery with a smile. Without much effort Hershel pushes the loft ladder back up into place. As Hershel brushes the dust off his t-shirt his mother walks around the corner into the hallway. She notices her son's face is white and his body shaking and sweating.

"What were you doing up there?" his mother asks in a sharp, loud and deep tone purposely meant to scare her son, if just a little.

Hershel jumps as he lets out a frightened squeal before trying to compose himself. Now shaking uncontrollably, he responds, "Just looking at grandpa's stuff, nothing really, lots of old clothes and this *tallit* which I want to look at while I'm here."

Hershel looks at his mother. She notices the long *tallit* but thinks nothing of it. She pats her son on the back of the head and smiles as he walks past her to go downstairs.

Hershel enters the guest room closing the door behind him. He leans back resting the back of his head against the closed door and rests his eyes. He turns around and presses his ear against the back of the door to listen and make sure his mother hasn't followed him. It's all clear. He walks quickly and places the *tallit* on the desk.

Again, he begins to pace around the room. There's no going back now. Hershel eventually moves his backpack from the chair and sits down. He turns on the desk lamp and now has plenty of light to see the object clearly. He carefully removes the stick from the *tallit* and is stunned. It's beautiful, very old, black, smooth and hard – just as his grandfather had described it. Hershel's thoughts quickly turn to disbelief that the object actually exists. His nerves return as he again recollects his promise. Holding it in his hands the black petrified wooden stick continues to shine under the desk lamp. As he slowly turns the stick, the orange glass, imbedded in the knot, glistens under the artificial light. Thunder and lightning break the silence again. Hershel stands to look out the window, the storm is getting closer. He wraps the object in the *tallit* and leaves it on the desk. Hershel walks backwards unable to take his eyes off the *tallit* and falls backward to sit on the bed. He is exhausted after the search and his sleepless night. It's been a long and emotional few days but they will pale in comparison to the journey ahead.

3

The old rabbi

The late morning sun glances under the curtains in the guest room. A sliver of warmth shines on Hershel's face as he wakes from another restless night. He twists and turns before thoughts of yesterday trigger him awake. Hershel quickly sits upright like he's been called to attention. After much thought overnight, Hershel has decided to fulfil his grandfather's wish to visit the old rabbi to see what he makes of the black stick. Hershel makes his way downstairs to the kitchen and notices his parents are out. Breakfast is unfamiliar territory but given it's available in the house he loads the toaster with four slices of bread and sits at the table. Hershel begins to Google the details of the old rabbi and the New York synagogue on his cell phone.

Hershel first met old Rabbi Manassah as a child but in recent times had not been close to his faith. He easily finds the phone number and nervously calls the synagogue.

"Hello?" A lady answers.

"Hello, my name is Hershel Rosen and I would like to speak with Rabbi Manassah please?" he asks in a shy schoolboy-like manner.

"Please hold," a Yiddish voice asks politely.

Unsure how long he will be on hold, Hershel looks back at the toaster in two minds whether to get up and check if it's ready or stay at the table.

Suddenly the old rabbi responds. "Hello, hello this is Rabbi Manassah."

"Hello, rabbi, ah…shalom, I guess. I am Hershel, my grandfather was Gregory Shapiro and he asked me to meet you just before he passed away," Hershel explains quickly and quietly, his lack of confidence evident to the old rabbi.

"Oh yes, *Baruch Dayan Emet*," the rabbi gives his condolences in Hebrew.

"I would like to meet as soon as possible, maybe later today?" Hershel's tone changes to one of urgency.

"I understand, I met your grandfather once, we had an interesting discussion. Let's see, I can meet this afternoon at three o'clock. You go to college as I recall, can we meet in the library?" the rabbi calmly suggests.

"Yes, yes, the front of the library at three o'clock, thank you rabbi, I will see you then," Hershel politely confirms and ends the call.

Hershel sits back in his chair as the next step in his grandfather's quest has now been secured. He turns on the television. As his toast pops up behind him, he ignores the sound and focuses on the television news which is dominated by the looming United Nations vote for the establishment of the Council for Religious Coexistence. The reporter is interviewing an American diplomat and prominent Jewish businessman named Isaac Goldberg who has just announced his intention to accept his nomination for the role of under-secretary for the new council. Hershel is watching but not listening closely as his mind is elsewhere. He begins to write a note for his parents letting them know that he will return to his apartment in the city for the day but be back for dinner. He turns off the television and returns to the guest room to shower and change. As he leaves the house, the toast remains in the toaster, hard and cold. Hershel makes his way down the street to catch the bus back to his apartment. His backpack has an umbrella holder on the side and it nurses an umbrella cover with the *tallit* and stick inside.

The bus stops a block before Hershel's apartment and he steps off. Now hungry, he walks to a nearby deli where he orders a sandwich and drink. He notices that the staff and patrons in the deli are all watching and listening to the television at the voting for the new UN council. Whilst it's huge news Hershel continues to eat his sandwich, looking the odd man out as he is the only person facing away from the television.

Hershel finishes his lunch and looks at his watch before leaving the deli and walking the relatively short distance to his apartment.

Hershel walks into the apartment and greets his flatmate who is also watching the television coverage of the United Nations council vote.

"Can you believe this Hershel, this is a huge step towards peace, no more wars," his flatmate says excitedly but he gets no reaction from Hershel.

As Hershel makes his way to his room and puts his backpack on the bed, he places the umbrella cover on his desk and carefully removes the *tallit* and its black stick. He gently folds the *tallit* and places it in a self-seal plastic bag and stores it in a desk drawer. He rolls the black stick in a towel and carefully inserts it back into the umbrella cover and places it on the side of his backpack as before. He notices the time and grabs his bike from his room. He lets his flatmate know he is heading to the library to study. His flatmate lets out a grunt in acknowledgement.

As Hershel rides through the streets of New York he is surrounded by conflict. On one street two Italian men are involved in a road rage incident, on another street police are arresting an African man unwilling to cooperate with everything he is told to do. On the next street two middle aged men shout at each other, and across the street a hooded man is running out of a store holding a gun and bag being chased by two Asian store employees yelling to everyone that they've been robbed. No one acts, no one cares.

As Hershel approaches the library, he sees Rabbi Manassah traditionally dressed and standing at the front steps. There is no mistaking he is a rabbi. At his feet a bloated backpack. As Hershel approaches Rabbi Manassah raises his hands to the skies.

"It's too beautiful a day for an umbrella, no?" the rabbi shouts humorously.

Hershel returns the comment with a smile as he dismounts and locks his bike in the rack on the library steps. He nervously greets the old rabbi and shakes his hand. Despite the fact Hershel is already carrying his backpack, the rabbi instructs Hershel to also carry his bag which Hershel struggles to lift.

"What have you got in here, the ten commandments?" Hershel asks smartly.

The old rabbi grabs Hershel's elbow and leads him quickly into a quiet corner of the library. Both men look around like CIA agents trying to find a quiet table. Before long they sit as Hershel drops both bags on the floor and sits down to catch his breath.

"Thank you for seeing me Rabbi Manassah." Hershel says, relieved.

The old rabbi nods as he grabs Hershel's wrist.

"I am pleased to be here with you Hershel and again my condolences on the passing of your grandfather," he says in a soft, calming and caring voice.

"Thank you, thank you rabbi. Do you know why I'm here?" Hershel struggles to complete his comments and is forced to take a deep breath.

The old rabbi sits back and looks at Hershel with a little nod of his head as Hershel continues the questions.

"Okay," Hershel pauses. "Did my grandfather ever tell you any war stories or anything about serving with the Israeli Army, especially on the Gaza Strip?"

Immediately Rabbi Manassah focuses on the concern on Hershel's face.

"Yes, yes, he did but that was a long, long time ago," the old rabbi replies.

Hershel interjects and reaches down to grab the umbrella cover. He places it on the table and takes the cover off revealing the towel which he begins to unwrap.

"Very unlucky to open an umbrella indoors my son," The rabbi jokes.

Hershel slowly removes the towel to unravel the black stick.

"Did he ever tell you or show you this black stick with the orange glass?" Hershel asks having no idea of what he has just revealed in public.

The old rabbi's eyes light up and he immediately covers the black stick with the towel. He takes a deep breath and is in shock. His mouth opens before his hands nervously rub his nose, eyes and cheeks in every direction.

"Be quiet, keep your voice down," the rabbi whispers as he frowns and stands to look around the library for any undesirable spectators. He wipes his forehead with his hand and sits back down. He slowly takes the towel off and reveals the black stick. The old rabbi glances at Hershel who can see the exhilaration evident across the old man's wise but weathered face. The rabbi carefully begins to examine the black stick but is careful not to touch it.

"Shapiro told me a story about this but it was just a story. I never got to see what he was talking about. He promised to show me one day but we never got to meet again. I have waited and hoped for this day since he and I first met." The old rabbi's comments are a mix of sadness and joy as this once mythical black stick is actually real and on display before him. Immediately he notices the orange glass in the knot. He retracts his fingers from that area like it's red-hot, careful not to touch it. He is well aware of the legend behind the story. He looks at the glass and quickly pulls his eyes away. Hershel is startled at the old rabbi's reaction.

"What is it rabbi, you know more don't you?" Hershel whispers nervously as he too stands slightly to look around the empty library for undesirable people, though uncertain who he should be worried is actually listening in.

The old rabbi's face changes to a serious and scared pale complexion as he conducts a closer inspection of the orange glass which he identifies as amber located at the lower end of the old black stick.

"Do you know what you have here?" the old rabbi whispers back.

Hershel is shaking his head wanting to know more while the old rabbi continues, not bothering to wait for a response. The rabbi reaches into his backpack and pulls out an old Bible from what appears to be a mini-library in his backpack. He places the book on the table and frantically flicks through the pages until he comes to an illustration in the Old Testament. The image is that of Moses holding the Ten Commandments at Mt Sinai with the burning bush in the background and his Staff resting upright on a nearby rock face. The old rabbi turns the book around and points to the image as he shows Hershel. Hershel studies the image in the book carefully then looks at the old rabbi before his attention returns to the image.

"Moses?" he says not quietly enough.

"Shhh," the rabbi nervously exhales with his hands extended slightly instructing Hershel to keep his voice down.

Again, Hershel stands slightly to look around the library, there is still no one.

"You know what this is?" asks the old Rabbi repeatedly tapping his finger on the picture of Moses like he is sending Morse code.

Hershel doesn't make the connection. The old rabbi then points to the Staff in the picture, which is double the size of the old black stick on the table in front of him. Hershel again shakes his head.

"The Staff rabbi, Moses' Staff?" Hershel whispers unsure of his utterance.

The rabbi nods his head.

"Rabbi, the Staff of Moses is on display at Top Kapi Palace in Istanbul, I studied that," Hershel states.

The rabbi lifts his head. "Ha, reputedly my son, reputedly. It is also alleged to be on display in the Egyptian Gallery of the Birmingham Museum in England. How do you explain that?" The rabbi continues, explaining the history of the Staff.

"In our faith Hershel, the Staff of Moses was passed down through history. The first owner was Adam who found this Staff in the garden of Eden. Adam then passed it down and so on and so on until it came into the possession of Moses. Regarding its existence and location today, it is also just as plausible that the Staff was destroyed by invading armies and left in pieces and if so, what better place for the Staff to be found than in the Holy Land, by a Jew, during a war."

The rabbi lowers his arms, tired from their excessive waving while explaining everything to Hershel. As Hershel pays closer attention to the image in the old Bible, the rabbi begins to explain further pulling another book from his bag.

"Here, the Midrash tells us the Staff was passed down from generation to generation and was in the possession of the Judean kings until the First Temple was destroyed." The rabbi pulls yet another book out of his bag and raises his hand in the air and excitedly explains:

"In Samuel I, 17:40, it is said concerning King David: 'And he took his Staff in his hand according to Midrashic tradition.' This is a reference to Moses' special Staff. It is unknown what became of the Staff after the Temple was destroyed and the Jews were exiled from their land. Maybe the Staff was destroyed too and that's why you only have half of it?"

The rabbi finishes his brief summary then begins madly typing into his iPad.

Hershel notices the iPad and looks at the old rabbi surprised and impressed that he has embraced technology but wondering why then he needed the big bulky books.

"You like my tablet?" the old rabbi asks. "You know the first Jew to download a file from the cloud to a tablet was Moses." He slaps Hershel's arm and laughs cheekily to ease the tension.

Hershel doesn't crack a smile and shakes his head dismissing the bad joke. Hershel is transfixed by the image in the Bible and the black stick on the table in front of him. He notices what he has is half the size of the illustration and dumbly asks,

"Can I, you know part the...Hudson River if I only have half of it rabbi?"

The old rabbi holds up his iPad and shows Hershel his Google search, a post from Rabbi Menachem Posner commenting that it is unknown what became of Moses' Staff after the temple was destroyed and the Jews exiled from their land.

"You shouldn't do anything with it," the old rabbi warns Hershel.

Hershel is in disbelief not yet realising what his grandfather stumbled upon that day in Gaza. Again, the rabbi holds open the Old Testament pages of the Bible with the image of Moses holding his Staff and turns the page to another photo showing Moses using the Staff to part the Red Sea. Concerned that Hershel has not understood the gravity and enormity of what he possesses, the old rabbi issues a very clear warning. "I have explained to you what you have, I have not explained the divine power you now hold."

The nervous old rabbi looks deep into Hershel's eyes and continues.

"You have *the* most powerful ritual instrument known to man in your hands. It is responsible for awe inspiring and nature taming miracles never before seen and never seen since by man. It summoned the 10 plagues of Egypt, including turning the Nile red, and when dropped before Pharaoh it became a snake before his very eyes. This Staff led the Exodus and freed the Israelites from slavery, parted the Red Sea and drowned Pharaoh's pursuing army. It struck a rock and brought forth a mineral spring to quench the thirst of Israelites in the desert searching for the promised land."

The rabbi looks deeper at Hershel whose eyes have not left the rabbi's worried face. The rabbi is still not convinced Hershel has acknowledged the seriousness and power of the Staff so he continues.

"This is a conductor of divine power transformed by God himself at the burning bush. It was owned by the founder of the Israelite religion."

It is then the rabbi notices a change in Hershel, he is wide-eyed and his head falls into his hands in worry. Hershel's newfound responsibility has dawned on him. The rabbi finishes his warning by picking up the Bible and pointing to the images.

"Look at these pages Hershel. The events documented here were lived and witnessed by thousands and today they are believed and adored by millions."

Hershel is in awe and begins to comprehend the power of the Staff. He finally responds slowly, nodding his head at the old rabbi.

"I will not let you down rabbi."

Hershel begins to wrap the towel around the Staff and stands as he prepares to leave. The old rabbi motions to Hershel to sit back down which Hershel does without hesitation.

"I've not yet told you about the orange glass in the knot," the rabbi says.

"Legend states the knot in the Staff was filled with sap and instantly forged into amber during Moses' encounter with the burning bush." Again, the old rabbi pulls out another book from his backpack and places it on the table which is quickly running out of room. The rabbi continues, explaining to Hershel how the Staff came to be in its current form. He explains that Jesus of

Nazareth briefly came across the Staff and that he chose his disciples by looking through the amber. In doing so, the seer would be able to confirm the purity of their souls. Hershel is now confused.

"When you look through the amber, those who appear on the other side became Jesus' advocates, his disciples," the old rabbi explains.

Hershel's mouth is now dry, and he wonders how many more warnings will there be. Flashes of regret appear on his face. What has he gotten himself into? How can this hugely historically relevant object be in *his* possession?

The old rabbi finishes by issuing a final warning. "What I am about to say is very important Hershel, more important than everything else I have explained today." The worried look on the old rabbi's face worries Hershel. The old rabbi holds Hershel's wrists.

"It is believed that by looking through the amber those who do not appear on the other side are deemed sinners and will suffer in the Gehinnom, or as we know it, a place that, well isn't like heaven." The old rabbi sits back looking at the library ceiling as silence falls all around.

Hershel is in awe and begins to grasp the quantum of power contained in the Staff. The Rabbi grabs Hershel's wrist again.

"This is the most important part and never forget this. Some believe, by pressing the amber the Staff possesses the power to perform a 'divine' act. When you press the amber those around you, in close proximity, those who the Staff has already identified as condemned are sent immediately to the afterlife, I mean right there and then. Do you remember your grandfather's story? The skirmish ended the moment he rubbed the glass and soldiers and civilians died on the spot. Do you understand?" The old rabbi whispers before footsteps force him to stop speaking.

Hershel is in total disbelief as he looks at each of the books and iPad open on the table. He failed to make the black stick connection in his grandfather's story. The old rabbi stands and looks around searching for the person responsible for the footsteps. While the rabbi is distracted, Hershel picks up the Staff and looks through the amber at the old rabbi. He clearly sees the old rabbi on the other side surrounded by a strange heavenly aura. The old rabbi turns his attention back to Hershel and with ninja-like speed snatches the Staff away with one hand and slaps Hershel lightly across the head with the other forcing Hershel to lower his head.

"This is not a toy or a game son!" the old rabbi says sharply before remembering where he is and sits back down.

Hershel places the Staff back on the table. The old rabbi takes out his cell phone and begins taking photos of the Staff from every angle making notes of its length and width and again warns Hershel.

"You must be careful now, powerful people will be after this, after *you* if they find out you have it. For us, the Staff has always been a symbol of hope, freedom and kindness but for others like Pharaoh and the Egyptians in the time of Moses, it was a symbol of misery, darkness and evil."

Hershel acknowledges the old rabbi's final warning and starts wrapping up the Staff with the towel before placing it into the umbrella cover. Hershel stands to leave and looks back at the old rabbi whose hands are nervously rubbing his face again. The old rabbi is overwhelmed and in a state of amazement as he mutters unintelligibly to himself in Hebrew.

"I will look after it rabbi, I promise you like I promised my grandfather," Hershel assures the old rabbi as he rests a hand on his shoulder.

As Hershel walks away the rabbi studies the images of the Staff he now has on his cell phone and begins returning his books to his backpack. He pauses and watches Hershel walk away.

"Guard and guide that boy Lord," he mutters in Hebrew.

4

Isaac Goldberg and the United Nations

The persistent sound of a hammer repeatedly hitting a gavel calls to order a noisy and disorganised meeting of the United Nations General Assembly. The frustrated Deputy Secretary-General's desperate pleas for calm go unnoticed. He shakes his head at the excited behavior of certain representatives, mainly those from countries whose foundations are based and driven by religious beliefs. Israel for example, Islamic driven nations like Malaysia and Indonesia and Christian centres like America and Britain. There are newly established countries – Independent Islamic State now owns half of Pakistan. The Shiites and Sunnis are also present. Despite the unruly behaviour, there is a good feeling in the assembly today.

As the deputy calls for silence once more, the Secretary-General steps towards the podium nervously scanning the representative filled room. He waits for calm before composing himself to make a statement.

"A recorded vote has been requested," he begins, pausing to study the result on a sheet of paper. "I am pleased to announce Draft Resolution AR75 to create a fifth council of the United nations, the Council for Religious Coexistence was adopted by a vote of 101-57."

Cheers erupt with a small number of representatives mumbling their disapproval.

The Secretary-General continues. "I shall now call on those representatives who wish to nominate candidates for the new council to stand and address the assembly. I should like to remind representatives that explanations of the nominations are limited to 10 minutes and should be made from your position and not the podium."

Immediately, the United States representative stands and speaks.

"The United States and countries of the United Kingdom nominate Mr Isaac Goldberg for the position of under-secretary-general of the new council."

The assembly fills with thunderous applause. Goldberg is one of only a handful of nominees, none of whom are as experienced and devoted as Goldberg. Isaac Goldberg is a prominent Jew and political statesman and a very successful businessman in his younger days. The shortish bespectacled Goldberg with his speckled grey hair stands as the assembly applauses. The United States representative waits for the applause to die down before delivering a prepared speech justifying Goldberg's nomination which includes his achievements, experience and qualifications. As his nomination speech ends the assembly applauds again.

In a gesture of good faith, and totally unexpected, the representative from Palestine seconds the nomination which is met with thunderous applause from the General Assembly. The actions of Palestine are seen as a huge step forward, a sign that perhaps all nations are seeking long-term peace.

Goldberg's face lights up as he is congratulated by his fellow countrymen and surrounding representatives from other countries who make their way to Goldberg to also shake his hand. Inspired by the actions of the Palestinian delegation, one by one each nation agrees with the nomination. As more people move to congratulate Goldberg, his face changes from one of joy and satisfaction to a wry smile as the enormity of the responsibility sinks in. Isaac Goldberg is a hardened man. He has worked his way through the United States' and international political systems to get to the position of under-secretary. There are many things he has condoned which others would condemn but Goldberg isn't bothered, he is an ambitious man.

With another vote amongst the representatives it becomes official – Goldberg has secured enough votes and is appointed to the position of under-secretary-general.

The media is invited into the room as the race begins to secure the first photos and interview of new Under-Secretary Goldberg who thrives on the attention. This is a big step forward and one step closer to his goal of UN Secretary-General.

Goldberg arrives at his New York home and is greeted by his small black dog at the front door. He walks into the kitchen where his wife is standing at the bench finishing a glass of champagne. Next to her, a glass for Isaac and an open bottle nestled in a sterling silver ice bucket. She picks up both glasses and begins to fill them before handing one to her husband. She is watching CNN and looks into her husband's eyes and begins to cry. They gently fall into a happy and warm congratulatory embrace.

"This could change the world Isaac," she whispers between tears.

"I know, I know, it's a very big step forward for me, for us *neshama*, for the world," Goldberg, calling his wife sweetie in Hebrew, replies emotionally.

Goldberg's mother and father, who were waiting in the living room, walk into the kitchen, cheering and shouting *mazel tov*, a traditional Hebrew congratulation. Goldberg hugs his parents and he immediately notices the look of delight on his father's face. Goldberg's wife ushers everyone into the dining room. It is Shabbat, a weekly holy night for Jewish families, and everyone sits for the Friday evening ritual.

Over dinner Goldberg's father raises his glass to toast his son.

"Isaac, my boy, congratulations on your appointment. You have worked very hard and we are very proud of you," Goldberg's father declares, only just managing to hold back tears.

It is the first time Goldberg recalls his father openly expressing his pride. They all raise a glass, some smile, some shed a tear on what becomes an enjoyable and memorable night for the family.

As always, after dinner the men retire to the study. Both sit in silence. Goldberg's father scans the room which is surrounded by timber bookshelves filled with leather-bound books. The study is finely furnished with two Chesterfield lounges facing each other and the most ornate antique desk. Goldberg's father has been in the study before but is always in awe of the room before commenting proudly to his son, "A United Nations under-secretary-general. This is a big responsibility you have my son."

Goldberg nods in acknowledgement as he prepares two glasses of scotch, handing one to his father before joining him on the opposite couch.

"I mean you have the power to negotiate, find and keep peace, to decree that all religious conflicts be resolved by discussion and the possibility that wars become a thing of the past. The world has never seen anything like this. You have great power but do you also have a force at your disposal?" Goldberg's father asks in a concerned tone unsure of the support available to his son.

"Yes dad, we will see. We still need to work out the terms of reference, our jurisdictions, resolution methodology, many things," Goldberg responds looking at the worry on his father's face.

His father notices a look emerge across his son's face that he's never seen before. He knows his son is more than capable of doing the job but it has its dangers and uncertainties. Should the council fail then the world will lose any hope of peace for some time, not to mention the failure will fall fairly and squarely on his son's shoulders. Both men continue their long overdue conversation before finishing their scotch and retiring for the night.

A month goes by and a beautiful blue sky covers the UN headquarters building in New York. A shiny limousine with clean and crisp UN flags proudly flying on its front side panels approaches before stopping at the front steps. Media from around the world surround the vehicle as Under-Secretary-General Isaac Goldberg steps out waving to the crowd. The large press contingent begins to launch numerous questions which fly through the air unanswered.

Goldberg stops to make a statement. "Thank you, this is a wonderful day for the UN and the world. We will be working hard on cementing our decision-making processes and other protocols over the next few weeks, again thank you."

Goldberg continues on through the media scrum eventually entering the building where he is greeted by his newly appointed executive assistant Emily.

"Good morning sir," she says confidently.

As big an opportunity as this appointment is for Goldberg it is also a great opportunity for Emily. Her years of service at the UN have paid off with this promotion, her first senior administrative position for a high-ranking UN executive. She is smart, sharp, young and gorgeous giving her a distinct advantage in an organisation still dominated by middle aged, dark suited men. She is also of the Jewish faith which Goldberg finds convenient as he doesn't have to explain why he is absent at certain times for Jewish events and holidays. As the pair walk towards the elevators Emily shows her efficiency by wasting no time in briefing Goldberg on the agenda for the day.

"Mr Goldberg, today we will be preparing for the first meeting and reviewing the running sheet for the meeting, establishing a structure for the post-meeting media briefing and formal communications, including agreed actions, to the UN."

Goldberg is very impressed with her competency and the pair make their way into Goldberg's office which is nothing short of magnificent with wonderful views of New York's East River and modern furnishings. Emily, who Goldberg calls Em for short, continues her brief of the day's events, specifically the council meeting.

"Mr Goldberg, we first welcome the representatives, then we thank the nations for your election followed by the major part, your opening address and your intended approach to achieving the goals and objectives of the council." Goldberg nods and replies, "Perfect Em. Now you work on the welcome and final thank you and I'll work on the methods and my initial address okay?"

They both smile at each other before Em leaves the office. Goldberg opens his briefcase and removes the notes he has already prepared for his address and the council's modus operandi. He reviews what he has written over and over again. He is a perfectionist, immersing himself in his notes constantly making small changes. He stands and walks toward the large window to appreciate the view before beginning to practice the hand gestures he will be using during his address. He pauses to take in the view. He is ready, but he reflects for a moment, he has always been ready for this appointment.

An hour or so later Emily knocks on the office door. "It's time sir, do you have everything?"

Goldberg nods as Emily hands him the document she was responsible for preparing. The pair make their way out of the office to the elevators and head to the meeting. Along the way Goldberg shakes hands with many UN representatives and staff who continue to congratulate him and wish him luck. He enters the auditorium where the council meeting will take place and makes a special effort to continue to shake hands with as many representatives as possible as it is their support he will be seeking and needs throughout the next few months. Eventually, Goldberg takes his seat and instructs the deputy to call the meeting to order. The deputy then invites Goldberg to welcome the representatives and open the inaugural meeting. Goldberg begins his address:

"Distinguished guests, ladies, gentlemen, my brothers and sisters.

I want to begin by thanking the High Representative for the United Nations Alliance of Civilizations, Mr Kwiata, for arranging this important occasion. I also commend the Government of Spain – and particularly its Foreign Minister Mrs Maria Vicente – for her initiative and extensive efforts in gathering the many religious leaders from around the world here for the inaugural meeting of the United Nations Council for Religious Coexistence."

The assembled representatives applaud to acknowledge the work of the people so far mentioned in Goldberg's address. Goldberg continues:

"Allow me to extend a very warm welcome to all of you and to express my humble thanks for your support in electing me under-secretary-general.

I am tremendously inspired and uplifted by your selfless willingness to come together around our shared hope and united commitment to building peace and tolerance. I very much look forward to working closely with you all."

Again, Goldberg pauses as the representatives applaud before continuing.

"In taking up this solitary role, I am only too aware of the obligations entrusted to me as under-secretary-general and of my responsibility for the faithful discharge of the duties appropriated to this appointment.

"In undertaking our collective responsibilities as a council of the United Nations, we have an expectation from the people of all nations to engage wholeheartedly in the achievement of that elusive concord which we all desire and which the world has not yet been able to achieve.

"The challenge before us is compelling and I call on all of us, as leaders of religion, from this very moment onwards, to imprint indelibly in our actions and in our hearts the sacred aim for *peace* and *tolerance* and the elimination and sure end to existing conflicts born of religious convictions and other mercenary and worthless motivations."

Thunderous applause from the representatives interrupt Goldberg's words.

UN staff and media who have filled the auditorium also join in. Goldberg continues.

"In working together to design, construct and document what we must do, it is important to remember and place at the core where our world has been for what seems an eternity. I ask you to bear in mind that over the past 3400 years, humans have been entirely at peace for only 268 of them. In recorded history there have been 123 wars that fundamentally originated from religious motives. As far back as the Mesopotamian Ages people have fought one another over one religious dispute or another, often because they believed that their god was guiding them to engage in conflict, regardless of sense or reason, in order to conquer land and build their nation.

"Around 1500 BC, while they searched for the promised land, the Israelites saw to take Canaan. I mention this event as here the Israelites, beyond just motivation, also used in battle, the first ever weapon of mass destruction against their fellow man. This was a ritualistic instrument called the Ark of the Covenant to lead their army, causing the walls of Jericho to crumble.

Before long we had the Roman persecution of early Christians. In 624 AD, the Arabic or Islamic conquests and the battle for Mecca. In 1095 the Crusades and the conquest of Arabs in the Holy Land. 1478 the Spanish Inquisition and in 1531 the Second War of Kappel between Catholics and Protestants in Switzerland.

"In 1562 we had the French Religious Wars, again between Catholics and Protestants, and the same again in the late 1960s and 1970s with conflict in Northern Ireland. 1966 saw the Buddhist Uprising in Vietnam against the Catholic-led government and in 1975 the Lebanese Civil War between the Shiites and Sunnis. Sadly, gravely, there are many, many more and I am, quite frankly, too heartbroken and fearful to mention them.

In every corner of the world, on almost every continent, throughout history and for whatever reason, religious wars occurred."

Goldberg pauses to compose himself.

The representatives are silent, ashamed of the human race.

Goldberg supresses his emotions before continuing.

"Today I call on the council member nations present and to my fellow representatives here to keep in mind the over one billion men, women and children, both military and civilian, guilty and innocent, who gave up their lives in religious and other conflicts. I call on you to respect them, to honour their legacy spanning many centuries, by making a commitment right here and now to trust the process upon which this council is about to embark to change the world for good, for always."

The auditorium respectfully stands and applauds Goldberg's words. He encourages the attention and makes no attempt to restore order. He'll take all the praise he can get right now. The moment he senses the crowd ease off he motions for them to sit before instructing the deputy to call the meeting to order. As the deputy stands and announces the meeting agenda, the first of which is to agree on the goals of the council, he attempts to read out the first goal but is immediately interrupted when an objecting representative yells, "There is no God but Allah."

Clearly not the start anyone wanted as the comment is met with both support and condemnation from different representatives. Goldberg is forced to stand and plead with the representatives to respect the deputy and pleads for decorum in order for the deputy to record the agreed goals and objectives. The deputy thanks Goldberg and continues.

"The first objective is the identification of lands currently being contested and to divide or yield relevant lands as agreed by majority vote of this council."

The auditorium erupts with rage. They do not disagree with the objective of resolving territorial disputes but the pain of the past and centuries of suffering endured by various religious groups. Specific incidents are aired to justify their quest for, and right to, the land.

The difficult meeting continues with constant interruptions from representatives triggering emotions in others demanding to be heard out of turn in an attempt to establish their place in some strange pecking order. Others speak simply to be seen as controversial, to make a name for themselves or impress by attracting media attention. There are threats of violence and the meeting is called to order far too many times. Clearly Goldberg and his team have lost control and adjourn the session early in the hope of a better outcome tomorrow.

Goldberg leaves the auditorium and looks at Emily in disbelief. The pair walk back to Goldberg's office where Emily prepares a glass of scotch. Goldberg grabs the scotch and finishes it in one hit before making his way to his desk to sit down.

"Thanks, Em, I really needed that."

Emily smiles.

Goldberg paces the room thinking out loud with Emily.

"Do they really think they are going to convey their grievances to us and that we will consider them one by one and apportion a scoreboard value per hardship to calculate their entitlement for land like it's a game? That's not how this is going to work. It is going to take compromise and sacrifice to comply with a majority view, right?"

Goldberg looks at Emily who slightly shrugs her shoulders before responding.

"It will take time for them to realise that sir. This is the first session and there is well over a hundred, even a thousand years, of pain and religious based anguish to deal with. Maybe they thought this was the right time, you know, get in early and get things off their chest."

Goldberg calms down a little and informs Emily he is going home.

The next day the council meeting continues with a second session. Before long the session again quickly turns into mayhem. This time the representatives turn on each other with groups and countries trading insults. Whilst Goldberg tries to follow the agreed agenda, representatives from the most passionate countries clash with those representatives who it seems were there simply to improve their political status. Personal interest is placed before religious interest and worse still before what's in the best interests of the world. It's a huge step back from the giant leap forward the establishment of the new council provided and celebrated during the vote and the opening address. Again, the meeting adjourns for lunch earlier than expected. The media is having a field day and the story dominates the headlines.

Later in the afternoon the final session of the council meeting commences and Goldberg opens the session pleading for calm and professionalism amongst the representatives. He attempts to put forward a draft resolution, a speaking protocol when addressing the council. It is aimed at eliminating insults, no raised voices, no emotional outbursts and certainly no more tales of past injustices. Goldberg stresses that it is impossible to shape the future with so much legacy. He also hopes the resolution might lead to some agreement, proof that representatives can work together and achieve something, anything. Sadly, the voting is void due to key nations abstaining from the vote.

The council is dysfunctional. Goldberg is frustrated, he sees no way out of appeasing conflicted representatives and their respective countries. As insults again fill the air the sound of hammer on gavel ends the first council meeting. Goldberg is not interested in shaking hands and once out of the auditorium is hounded by the press wanting a statement. He ignores them and makes a quick exit.

Goldberg returns to his New York home. He walks into the kitchen where his wife is standing at the bench sipping on whisky. An empty glass and newly opened bottle sit alongside her waiting for Goldberg. A recently finished whisky bottle stands on an opposite kitchen counter. Goldberg looks at his wife and she begins to cry as they hug each other. He comforts her.

"We can't expect to resolve conflicts and beliefs that are thousands of years old in just three sessions he says softly.

She nods her head and responds, "I know but I can see this will take its toll on you, on us."

The couple hold their embrace silently for a few moments.

"What time are we expecting my parents for dinner?" Goldberg asks his wife as the front door bell suddenly rings. They look at each other and smile. It's Friday.

Dinner with Goldberg's parents is an ordinary and uninspiring occasion. Goldberg is disengaged and disconnected, his mind clearly consumed by the day's events. As usual after dinner Goldberg's father retreats to the study. Goldberg kisses his wife's forehead and takes his glass of whisky as he follows his father.

In the study Goldberg walks to his desk and flops into his chair. He notices his father staring at him.

"What is it dad?"

Goldberg's father seizes the opportunity to talk about his military service in Israel. He emotionally sets the scene of a particular patrol in Gaza. Goldberg can see his father is troubled and struggling to hold back tears. Goldberg has never heard his father speak of his military service before. Goldberg's father describes the details.

"Isaac, I need to tell you this story. A story about my service with the Israeli army in the Gaza Strip."

Goldberg tilts his head shaking it slightly to indicate his surprise and looks at his father. Why is this the time to talk about his army service? Why now? He asks himself.

Goldberg's father begins to tell the story of Shapiro, running alongside the tank and the civilian resistance in a small town in the Gaza Strip, the black stick and the imbedded orange glass. He recounts his side of the story and it differs little to Shapiro's tale with one exception – Goldberg's father is adamant that he found the black stick and asked Shapiro to simply hold it but Shapiro was obsessed with it and it never left his side even when he was recovering in hospital. When the two soldiers returned to base that day after the Gaza Strip episode, they never spoke of what happened. They did not include the incident in their reports. Shapiro was wounded and after being discharged from the army hospital was reassigned. Both men never served together on a mission nor saw each other ever again. After his national service, the search and understanding for the black stick became an obsession for Goldberg's father. In later years, Goldberg's father researched the old black stick; the length, the orange glass in the knot, its hardened age. He elaborates on the power he believes the black stick held in that it somehow ended the enemy engagement in Gaza that day.

Goldberg is staring at his father speechless, fascinated about the story while at the same time wondering if this is the first sign of old age, cognitive decline or mental instability in his ageing father. He finds it hard to believe what he is hearing. His father has never mentioned his military service nor any event, incident or location where he served. Goldberg continues to ponder, why this story and why now?

Goldberg's father reaches into his overnight bag and produces an old pocket Bible which smells stale and looks well worn, the spine and pages in tatters. Clearly, he has possessed this pocket Bible for some time. He moves to the desk and stands next to his son and opens the small book. Over 40 years of research notes are wedged throughout the small book like fragile bookmarks. The notes are dominated by stories of the Staff of Moses from early times to King David, sketches and drawings, and notes from meetings with various rabbis in Israel and the United States. Suffice to say Goldberg's father was consumed by the episode in the Gaza Strip.

Goldberg is amazed and puzzled. He looks at his father and stutters, "Is, is, is this real?"

"Yes, it is my son," his father replies. "After all my work I recently came to this conclusion. I believe this black stick we came across that day in Gaza was the Staff or part of the Staff of Moses. More importantly I know who has it or at least had it back then. I am getting older. I don't have the energy anymore to try and find him." Goldberg's father grabs his son's hand. "Isaac, I am certain I saw the Staff of Moses. Do you know what one could do with its power?"

Goldberg looks at his father and takes his hand away, his anger growing.

"Dad, what are you saying? "I don't have time to listen to fairytales and go on treasure hunts." Then it dawns on him.

"Oh, I see, you think I need...well, I don't need anything extraordinary to help me, especially something surrounded in religious sorcery. What will people think? I earned my position in the UN by sheer hard work and by being me and that's how I will lead." Goldberg quickly finishes what he has left of his scotch, he is tired and now feels insulted by his father.

"Look dad, let's talk more in the morning okay? It's great to have you and mum here tonight." Goldberg stands before kissing his father goodnight, placing a hand on his father's shoulder before he walks towards the study door.

"All my life, from when you were just a boy, I have, and will continue to, do anything in my power to not see you fail." Goldberg's father's makes his intentions very clear as his son leaves the room.

Goldberg's father is disappointed. He wonders whether he should have told his son earlier in his life or even told him at all? He also finishes his scotch followed by a cute tiny hiccup. Goldberg's father means well. He looks over his son's magnificent desk and pauses as a flash-back of that day in the Gaza Strip enters his thoughts. Clearly, those days still haunt him but he can endure no more. This is where his quest ends. Acknowledging that it's the right time to 'pass the baton' he places the old pocket Bible with all his notes in the top drawer of the desk and rests his hands on the leather desktop. His treasure hunting days are over. He has done all he can to track down this divine instrument. He chose this time to pass down his legacy to his son. He walks slowly towards the door and turns the lights off.

The next day Goldberg is in his study and contemplates ways to gain the co-operation of the council. Perhaps he needs to be stronger, maybe assert his authority to allow discussion, yes, but then propose a resolution soon after before emotions set in and the discussion escalates to unrest and disengagement. He then notices his desk drawer slightly ajar. As he opens the drawer there sitting on top of his papers is his father's old pocket Bible and accompanying notes. Goldberg removes the old book and closes the drawer. He places it on the desk and continues with his thoughts on council strategy.

Before long he is drawn to the pocket Bible and decides to flick through the pages. As he reads passages and notes, he can hear his father's voice. He comes across a small document which outlines his father's military service. It includes names of soldiers and serial numbers as well as when and where he served. He studies his father's papers all morning captivated by the numerous notes and the detailed information. Goldberg begins to contemplate that given the evidence before him the Staff and stories might be real. He blends his thoughts of council strategy with the possibility of possessing the apparent power of the Staff of Moses. After all, the Staff achieved great things for the Israelites. He decides that he at least owes it to his father to find out if the artefact his father found on the Gaza Strip that day really is the Staff of Moses.

Early Monday morning Goldberg calls Emily who is already in the office. He tells her there is a special research task he would like her to perform. Emily asks what it's all about and Goldberg tells her briefly that she will need to find an old Israeli Army veteran named Gregory Shapiro. He provides her with serial numbers and service record details. He instructs Emily to use every UN resource available to track down the old soldier. Goldberg finishes the call and ponders what's possible.

Nestled in his office at the UN, Goldberg again reflects on his frustration with the lack of progress at council. In preparation for next month's meeting he has resorted to having private discussions with the trouble-making representatives to attempt to understand their grievances and convince them that compromises will be required in order to broker some form of peace. He knows most of their demands are illogical and motivated by emotion and religious one-upmanship and nothing else. He is disturbed and angry by the lack of under-standing and the representatives' warped perspective of the council's title "religious coexistence."

Goldberg's thoughts are disrupted by an excited knock on the door.

"Come in Em," he says, already familiar with her quirky knock.

Emily enters smiling as she stands across the desk.

"Do you want the good news or bad news?" she begins excitedly in an attempt to cheer Goldberg up. In response a tired Goldberg just wants to know and sits back in his chair before motioning to Emily to tell him everything.

"Okay, sadly the first place you look for old people is the death notices so I searched for a Gregory Benjamin Shapiro with the date of birth you gave me, in the Israeli census records and came up with a man who migrated to the U.S. in the early 1970s. So, I then searched the US immigration records next." Emily says speaking quickly but thoroughly.

"Did you find him?" Goldberg replies, not interested in the effort but the result.

Emily shakes then nods her head.

"He changed his last name when he came to the U.S. but for some reason changed it back to Shapiro a few years ago. He passed away only two months ago."

Goldberg nods in acknowledgement as Emily continues.

"His death notice speaks of a daughter and as it was posted in New York. I think I can find her."

Emily smiles, pleased with her efforts.

Goldberg expected nothing less from Emily, he has heard nothing but good things about this hard working, reliable and trustworthy girl. He asks Emily to sit down and instructs her to find and possibly arrange a meeting with Shapiro's daughter. He instructs her to use his father's name as a soldier who served alongside Shapiro and ask questions about his life after Israel and his end of days.

Emily nods happily and asks, "What do you want me to talk to her about?"

Goldberg removes his father's old pocket Bible from his briefcase.

"Here is some light reading for you tonight Emily. It will be clear from the notes what I am after and why," he says softly as he hands the pocket Bible to her.

"This is confidential, only you and I need to know. All you need to do is find out whether Shapiro's daughter is aware of, or maybe has any let's say, 'recognisable' belongings, and the notes will clarify exactly what I mean." Goldberg's tone is serious and urgent.

Emily nods to Goldberg as she takes the pocket Bible with her. She is intrigued as she stands to leave the room.

Goldberg stands to look out his office window. His father's primitive investigative efforts were no match for today's finger-tip access to information and the powers of the UN. Goldberg is hopeful and smiles.

5

Hershel's success

In an old brownstone home in Harlem, New York, Emily is in her kitchen. She dumps her backpack on the floor and makes her way to the couch. Emily is intrigued by the old pocket Bible and its notes, and kicks off her shoes to get comfortable before lying on the couch. She flicks through the old pocket Bible and is instantly captivated. As she continues to turn each page, she meticulously studies both the scribble in the book as well as the notes intermittently wedged throughout. She immerses herself in sketches and drawings as well as notes from interviews with many rabbis done by Goldberg's father over the years. She doubts none of the old pocket Bible's contents. Hours go by and Emily is tired. She closes the old pocket Bible before tilting her head back on the couch. She closes her eyes and contemplates, what better time for the Staff of Moses to make an appearance than at a time when the world is gravely troubled, especially the new UN Council.

If Isaac Goldberg and his father believe the Staff is real and they know who has it and that it is within their reach, why not make every attempt to own it? Emily convinces herself that she wants to be part of the quest to ensure the Staff is found and ends up in the right hands. Emily closes her eyes and falls asleep.

The next morning, and with the power of the UN at her disposal, Emily wastes little time in trying to locate Shapiro's daughter. She makes a phone call to *The New York Times* newspaper and uses her status as well as her charm on a young administrator requesting the name and details of the person who placed Shapiro's death notice. She is prepared to wait on the phone for however long it takes and her patience pays off. The newspaper provides her with all the information, why wouldn't it? She is the executive assistant to a United Nations under-secretary. The information easily leads her to Mrs Rosen, Hershel's mother, and the family home in Syracuse. Emily thanks the young newspaper administrator and hangs up before picking up the phone and calling Mrs Rosen. Emily waits for the phone to answer.

"Hello," Mrs Rosen answers in a slow, soft tired voice.

"Hello Mrs Rosen, how are you?" Emily nervously begins.

"Yes, who is this please?" Mrs Rosen replies in a concerned tone.

"Hi Mrs Rosen my name is Emily, you don't know me but I am the executive assistant to Mr Isaac Goldberg. Do you know who Mr Goldberg is? He's been on the news." Emily drops a name to get Mrs Rosen's attention.

"Yes, Mr Goldberg, the new United Nations man?" Mrs Rosen asks.

"Yes, that's right Mrs Rosen. I am calling to let you know that Mr Goldberg's father served in the Israeli military with your father Gregory Shapiro. Did you know that?" Emily communicates the connection quickly to keep Mrs Rosen interested and open to meeting.

"Really, I did not know." Mrs Rosen's reply is short.

"Look Mrs Rosen, I am in New York at present and Mr Goldberg has asked me to meet with you and pass on his condolences on the passing of your father. If possible, could I come to your home this afternoon to drop off some flowers? As I said I am in New York today." Emily conveys the message sincerely.

Mrs Rosen is surprised but doesn't hesitate to accept the invitation, proud and grateful, especially coming from Goldberg, a man so prominent in the media.

"That would be wonderful my dear," she smiles.

"I have your address and will be there around three o'clock okay? See you then."

"That will be fine, see you then," Mrs Rosen replies and hangs up.

She then immediately calls her husband and Hershel to tell them the news. She asks both of them to be at home for the important meeting. Hershel offers to leave college early and come to the house. Mr Rosen has to stay at the office.

Emily is pleased with her progress, delighted with getting one step closer to the Staff. She returns to studying the details contained in Goldberg's father's notes. She comes across a hand-drawn map of the skirmish in the Gaza Strip including the location of the tank, the position of each soldier and the crumbling buildings where the civilians hid. There are drawings of the tank commander slumped over the turret and a soldier face down in the dirt which Goldberg's father has labelled 'Green'. She turns the page and comes across a sketch she has not seen before. A full-page image of a soldier marked Shapiro sitting on the ground leaning against the tank track wheels. She looks closer and notices he has no rifle or weapon of any kind. He is holding what looks like a stick. Emily is amazed as it appears Goldberg's father's story is definitely an eyewitness account and he has drawn the Staff of Moses. Emily closes the book leaving her finger on the page and takes a moment to comprehend the end game of the task she has been given. She also ponders the magnitude of what she has been asked to do and the significance of this artefact on the world and the Hebrew faith, after all she is Jewish. Emily returns to reading the notes picking up where she left off.

A stunning black limousine drives up a quiet tree-lined Syracuse street. Some residents are tending to their gardens and the appearance of the car turns heads while other neighbours peek out windows. The opulent vehicle is out of place in this community and certainly commands attention.

As the limousine approaches the Rosen house, Hershel and his mother are also peering through their front window in anticipation of the arrival of the UN executive assistant. They have been ready and waiting for an hour and are now excited at the sight of the jealous neighbours looking at the car approach the Rosen home. As the car stops in the Rosen driveway a chauffeur slowly emerges before immediately opening the rear door for Emily. As she gets out of the car, she stands on the driveway and briefly looks at the Rosen home before turning and noticing the neighbours up and down the street just staring. She asks herself how such a divine artefact has led her to such a simple and quiet location.

"Oh, she is so pretty Hershel," Mrs Rosen utters excitedly as Emily walks toward the front of the Rosen home. Hershel is silent, his mother is right, she is gorgeous. He reaches for his mother's hand and the pair walk out the front door and onto the porch to greet Emily who walks up the steps towards them holding a large bouquet of beautiful flowers. Hershel notices Emily is even more beautiful up close. He blushes and it doesn't go unnoticed.

"Come in my dear. Are those for me?" Hershel's mother takes the flowers.

"Hi Mrs Rosen, thank you so much for meeting with me," Emily greets the pair enthusiastically and shakes Mrs Rosen's hand.

Hershel smiles at Emily which she returns but with a puzzled look.

"Thank you, you're so lovely. This is my son Hershel," Mrs Rosen returns the comment with a smile.

Emily extends a hand to Hershel totally unaware of his existence; her research didn't go as far as identifying Shapiro's grandchildren, nor did she know he would be attending the meeting. Regardless, Emily hides her surprise. Hershel, stands tall and sucks in his stomach. With a pouted chest any peacock would be proud of he firmly returns Emily's handshake. He then notices a security officer standing guard at the limousine with the chauffeur. Emily picks up on Hershel's concern and attempts to break his stare.

"They're here simply as a UN precaution, standard procedure," she says dismissing the man's purpose.

Hershel has no reason to believe otherwise and nods his head.

"Come in sit down," says Mrs Rosen treating Emily like a daughter.

Hershel still hasn't said a word and with a hand gesture points to the front door as if to mime an invitation to Emily to enter the Rosen home. As he follows

Emily inside, he can't help but stare at her arse, it's perfect. Hershel's mother notices and elbows Hershel and smiles, lifting his jaw to close his mouth before it hits the porch timber floor. Hershel complains with a soft caveman-like grunt as Emily enters the home. All three make their way to the dining table. Mrs Rosen asks Emily whether she would like a coffee or tea.

"Coffee please, thank you…ah milk and no sugar," Emily responds.

Mrs Rosen then makes her way into the kitchen not bothering to ask Hershel, she knows how he has his coffee. Emily and Hershel sit at the table.

Emily is silent for a moment and stares nodding a little nervously at Hershel.

"So, Hershel, tell me about you? I know a little about your mother and grandfather of course but what about you, what's your story?" she asks with a captivating, brilliant smile.

Hershel is a bundle of nerves. He has never had a girlfriend or engaged in conversation with a girl let alone someone this smart and beautiful from the UN. He is impressed, way out of his comfort zone and clumsy. He attempts to swallow before responding but his mouth is dry. In a shaky voice, rapidly and in one breath, he blurts out, "Well, firstly I'm pleased to meet you too. I'm a huge fan of Under-Secretary-General Goldberg. You see I'm studying political science and have followed Mr Goldberg's success for some time."

Emily reaches over and touches his hand.

"You're a little nervous, I think I missed some of that," she giggles.

Hershel smiles, hoping it masks his excitement at the hand contact with Emily.

Hershel then nervously asks a question.

"You mentioned my grandfather and that's why you're here, right?"

Emily looks at him sharply but is interrupted as Mrs Rosen walks in with three coffees and a plate of biscuits for everyone.

"Yes…thank you Mrs Rosen. So, as I mentioned to your mother on the phone Hershel, the Goldberg family recently discovered that Mr Goldberg's father served with your grandfather in the Israeli Army," Emily responds confidently.

Hershel's face changes, he instantly makes the connection with Goldberg the soldier on the Gaza Strip that day. He hides his discovery well enough for Emily not to notice. Emily continues pointing to the large bunch of flowers.

"Firstly, Under-Secretary-General Goldberg wanted to pass on his condolences to you and your family as he was not aware of your father's passing Mrs Rosen."

Emily's gentleness warms the room.

Hershel looks at his mother face, it is filled with pride at the recognition.

Emily continues.

"Do you have any pictures of your father in the army Mrs Rosen? I'm sure Mr Goldberg and his father would love to see some?" Hershel looks blankly at his mother.

"Hershel, get your grandpa's photo album, the one from the attic. Hershel was a great help; he went through his grandfather's things in the attic not long after he passed away. I think he kept a uniform and helmet with some old Jewish things but the rest were old clothes which we donated and papers we threw away," his mother tells Emily in an appreciative tone.

Hershel is now nodding his head and speaks up.

"That's right, I kept the uniform and helmet upstairs."

Emily pretends to be thrilled – at least there are some belongings pertaining to Shapiro's time in the Israeli Army and asks to see the uniform so she can take pictures for Goldberg. As Hershel and his mother approve, Hershel steps away from the table and makes his way upstairs. Mrs Rosen smiles at Emily who seizes the opportunity of being alone with Mrs Rosen and focuses on the purpose of her visit.

"Thank you, Mrs Rosen, it would be wonderful to photograph those items. Could I ask you one more thing? Think back when you were going through your father's belongings, did you come across anything, like a military baton or ceremonial rod, it would have been the length of a cane or old umbrella?"

Mrs Rosen shakes her head as she responds, "I can't recall Emily, Hershel may know, he sorted the things in the attic for us."

At that moment Hershel walks in with the helmet, uniform and album. He kept them all in the guest room. He sees both women staring up at him, his cheeks go red before his mother asks, "Hershel, when you were in the attic that day did you notice a stick or a cane?"

Hershel's face freezes before slowly shaking his head. Emily notices the odd behaviour immediately. His secret is out. He carefully places the uniform, helmet and photo album on the table. Emily hoped her question went unheard by Hershel but it proved to be pivotal to her quest. Emily gives the Rosens a wry smile as she stands and snaps photos of the uniform and helmet with her cell phone and begins going through the photo album.

Hershel is worried and finds the courage to be assertive and asks, "Tell me more about this stick or cane that you're looking for?"

The smile disappears from Emily's face as she looks up at Hershel. It is clear he knows more but is giving up nothing. Emily doesn't push the issue and looks down to continue going through the photo album.

"Never mind, it's nothing really," she replies, dismissing the issue as unimportant.

Eventually, Emily comes across some military photos. She turns them around and notices Shapiro has written down the names of soldiers on the back of each photo. There are none that include Goldberg's father. Emily's cell phone rings.

"Excuse me for a minute please," she says as she stands and walks away from the table into another room.

Hershel looks at his mother who is still wallowing in delight at the bouquet of flowers. In no time Emily comes back to the table.

"So sorry Mrs Rosen but work calls and I have to get back to the UN building," she apologises,

"Oh, I understand, you're a very busy young lady. Please thank Mr Goldberg again," Mrs Rosen says charmingly.

All three make their way outside. As Emily says goodbye and thanks Mrs Rosen again, she walks down the porch stairs before turning back.

"Hershel, as part of your studies I could arrange a meeting with Under-Secretary Goldberg. Would you like that?" Emily cheekily sets a trap.

Hershel is over the moon and confirms his availability for the coming week.

Emily is equally pleased and tells Hershel she will call him in the next few days. Hershel thinks quickly.

"Oh, I don't live here, I'm in the city. Let me give you my card," Hershel clarifies, not wanting to miss the opportunity and hands over a coffee stained home-made business card that all nerds would of course possess.

Emily provides her business card in return and asks Hershel to call her in a few days. Hershel plays it cool but inside he is bursting. He got her number!

The Rosens wave at Emily as the car reverses out. As Mrs Rosen turns to face her home, she notices all the neighbours out on their manicured lawns staring at the shiny black car leaving the driveway. She cheekily waves at all of them feeling wonderful and important. Hershel stays on the porch staring down the street as Emily's UN car drives away slowly.

In the car Emily wastes no time calling Goldberg as she makes her way back to the UN building. She holds her cell phone waiting for an answer but has no opportunity to speak as Goldberg answers immediately.

"How did you go?" Goldberg asks in a tone Emily has not experienced before.

Emily's response is short.

"She has a son and I'm certain he knows where it is. He might even have it."

Goldberg pauses and instructs Emily to contact the son and arrange a meeting in a small café in the city in a few days' time. Emily acknowledges the instruction as the car drives out of the quiet suburb.

It's just after lunch and Hershel is in his apartment studying. It's been a few days now since he met Emily. He was so captivated that he can't remember if he was supposed to call her in a few days or she was going to call him. Beside his desk, the Staff is covered in the towel leaning upright. It rarely leaves his side. Hershel lifts his head and glances at the Staff, second-guessing why the UN lady was asking his mother questions about it. At that moment his cell phone rings.

"Hello?" Hershel answers uncertain of the caller.

"Hey Hershel, it's Emily." She is excited but calm and doesn't wait for Hershel to answer before she continues.

"Look we really didn't have a chance to talk, just you and I, so was wondering if we could catch up maybe this afternoon if you're free?"

Hershel jumps up from his desk, punches the air and paces around the room. He very quickly jumps to the conclusion that this is a date. Emily must like him otherwise she wouldn't have called so soon.

"Sure, that'd be good," he answers with a standard but shaky response – what would you expect from a nerd who's got a date with a beautiful girl?

His response appears to sound like he is playing it cool, but in his head and heart fireworks are going off.

Emily mentions the name of a café and Hershel lets her know that it's not far from his apartment. He is merely stating a fact but then thinks his comment about the close proximity of the café to his apartment might be misconstrued as being a little forward. Hershel tries to back-pedal and explain himself but he is interrupted by Emily who is giggling on the other end of the phone.

"Okay, I'll meet you there at three p.m.?" Emily coyly confirms.

Hershel dumbly nods not realising Emily can't see him as it's a phone call.

"That's fine Emily, see you then," he replies shyly.

Both say goodbye and wait for the other to hang up. They say goodbye again and Hershel hears Emily giggle as she hangs up.

An excited Hershel performs a small victory dance around his room executing a little ballet leap every now and then. He has a date for the first time in, well, ever. He sits back down and takes one look at his study notes on his laptop, he can't concentrate anymore. He needs new clothes and shoes. He grabs his backpack and heads off on his bike visiting clothing stores he has never set foot in before asking questions of every shop assistant of whether the clothes he is trying on make him look cool and attractive – to women, he clarifies. Hershel really wants this date to go well, he really likes this girl.

After five hours of shopping Hershel returns to his apartment. He enters his room dumping his shopping bags on the bed. The bags are filled with shirts, pants, a jacket and aftershave all of which he lays out neatly on his bed. He has a shower and gets ready for the date. Before long he is checking himself out in the mirror and he is looking good. He sprays the aftershave into the air and walks into it just like they showed him at the perfume counter. As Hershel walks out of his room his flatmate notices the pleasant smell and dumbly looks around trying to locate the origin of the scent. He is convinced it's some form of room deodouriser before realising it's Hershel.

"You look good buddy, but you stink," he states bluntly.

Hershel doesn't respond. He simply walks past him shaking his head as he guides his bike out the door. He heads out and makes his way to the café.

A UN security officer stands guard next to a black SUV sitting out the front of a café only two blocks away from Hershel's apartment. As he cycles down the street, he sees Emily standing at the café entrance. Hershel excitedly waves in a Forrest Gump like manner. It doesn't go unnoticed as Emily raises her hand a little then brings it back down to avoid further attention and embarrassment. As Hershel arrives, he parks and locks his bike before making his way to greet Emily.

"Hi Hershel, how are you?" Emily asks warmly.

She likes Hershel and in return he is transfixed by her beauty. Again, he notices the security by the car outside the café. The pair shake hands. Hershel is disappointed there is no other contact, no hug, no kiss on the cheek or touching of arms. Hershel wasn't really expecting any gesture of affection but it would have been nice if it happened.

As they approach the café entrance, Mark Wells, Head of UN Security and a good friend of Goldberg appears before raising his arm slightly as if to guide the pair to a table. Wells and Goldberg have been friends for some time as they commenced at the UN at the same time. Emily is uncomfortable with Wells as she walks past him into the café with Hershel in tow.

"You smell very nice sir," Wells says paying Hershel a creepy condescending compliment who doesn't know whether to reply or keep walking. Hershel keeps walking as he looks back oddly at Wells. As the pair walk through the café they come to a quiet corner. Hershel looks around and sitting at a table behind him is Isaac Goldberg.

Hershel is bewildered but pleasantly surprised. On the one hand he is meeting the one and only Isaac Goldberg, while on the other hand this is obviously not a date with Emily. He has no idea why Emily has arranged a meeting with Goldberg as that's not what she said on the phone. However, as a committed political science student, he is thrilled with the opportunity of meeting the very successful and prominent man.

Goldberg doesn't bother standing, he's all ego and filled with self-importance. Goldberg extends a hand to Hershel who also extends a hand thinking Goldberg is offering to shake hands. Just as Hershel reaches Goldberg's hand, it is withdrawn as Goldberg gestures for the pair to sit down. Hershel's arm is left extended and his hand hanging in midair. Hershel looks foolish and brings his arm down brushing his hand along the side of his jeans in an attempt to hide his embarrassment. Emily instructs Hershel to sit next to Goldberg. As he sits Hershel enthusiastically begins telling Goldberg how much of an honour it is to meet him. Goldberg nods with a wry smile and calls over a waitress who immediately makes her way to the table and takes the trio's order. As the waitress walks away, Goldberg wastes no time to get to the point.

"Glad you had the time to come here Hershel. Do you know why I wanted to meet you?"

Hershel shakes his head, looks at Emily then frowns.

Goldberg begins telling a story, a familiar story. One Hershel has only heard once before from his dying grandfather. The story is identical almost word for word, much to Hershel's amazement. Goldberg ends the story but it's not as Hershel remembers. "You see, my father found this black stick and he wants it back."

Goldberg's tone changes as he asks Hershel directly, "Do you know what I am talking about?" Goldberg has asked this sincerely, taking a chance that Hershel is the one who possesses the Staff.

Hershel pauses and looks at Emily before looking away at the security inside and outside the café. It is only then he realises the seriousness and importance of the meeting. Goldberg wants Hershel's attention and again asks the question, "Do you know where it is Hershel?"

Goldberg's tone is not as pleasant now.

Hershel turns his attention back to Goldberg and Emily and nods his head.

"I have it," he reluctantly discloses to Goldberg with a deep sigh.

Goldberg is amazed and sits back in his chair. His hunch pays off much to Emily's surprise.

As if the timing was choreographed the waitress arrives with their order. Goldberg was not really expecting that answer from Hershel. He really has hit the jackpot but hides his excitement well. Goldberg looks at Emily and is relieved he may be near the end of completing his father's quest to get back the Staff of Moses. All three thank the waitress as she walks away. Goldberg then leans forward and immediately re-emphasises to Hershel that his father found the Staff before Shapiro. He goes on stating that the only reason his father didn't keep it was that he was a young soldier and a very religious man and the Staff simply 'spooked' him. It's all lies and Hershel knows it. Goldberg's obsession with the Staff begins to bother Hershel as he remembers the rabbi's warnings.

Goldberg continues, saying it really didn't matter who found the Staff first and is grateful and praises Shapiro for looking after the Staff so well over such a long period of time. Goldberg thanks Hershel too for taking care of the Staff after Shapiro passed away. Hershel senses Goldberg's words are intended to convince him that Goldberg's father is the true owner of the Staff and he is simply thanking Hershel and his grandfather for fulfilling their role as mere caretakers. Hershel nods and attempts to speak when Goldberg interrupts: "I'll cut to the chase Hershel, I need the Staff son and am happy to pay you a good price for it." Goldberg points to security chief Wells, who is holding a briefcase.

"My people know everything about you Hershel, and as a student, the $2 million I am prepared to give you today will change your life and your family's life forever.

It is appropriate compensation, a reward if you like, for you and your family's efforts in keeping the black stick safe, don't you think?"

Hershel almost chokes on his coffee before Goldberg continues.

"This will help you and your family for all their hard work over the years Hershel. It's time to pass on that burden, that legacy to me and our family." Goldberg is sincere but demanding.

Hershel is amazed by the offer and thanks Goldberg. He sits back in his chair and asks whether he can take some time to think about the offer as thoughts fill his mind. He recalls his grandfather's words to 'keep it' and also the promise he made to the old rabbi to be careful about others knowing.

Goldberg sits forward and responds quickly but quietly. "Here's the thing Hershel, I know your apartment is not far away, that's why we are meeting here. Today my offer is $2 million, tomorrow my offer will be $1 million, the day after that who knows what the offer will be." Goldberg sits back in his chair.

Hershel feels cornered and looks at Emily. Concern appears on her face too.

Clearly, she was unaware of Goldberg's intentions. Goldberg continues.

"Hershel, your choice is to go back and get the Staff now and bring it to me here within the next hour or severely piss off a high-ranking member of the United Nations? Am I clear?" Goldberg smiles sarcastically.

Hershel is stunned. Goldberg has now called it 'the Staff' and must know the power it contains. Hershel looks up at the café ceiling then takes one look at Emily who shrugs her shoulders as an indication she had no idea about this deal or wants any part of it. Emily then nods which Hershel reads as a sign that it's a great offer and that Hershel should take it. Hershel nods back more so to please Emily.

"Okay, be right back," Hershel tells Goldberg before he jumps up from the table and walks out the café. In a rush, Hershel unlocks his bike and rides quickly.

"Follow him," Goldberg instructs Emily who instructs the security officer standing at the UN SUV to drive and follow Hershel.

Hershel cycles down the streets of New York trying to process what's happened and justify his decision. He mutters to himself, *I am not interested in what the Staff does or doesn't do. I am not religious. There are more important things in my life. The money will make all the difference and maybe that's why grandfather told me the story and where to find it. The old man would have done the same thing. I am betraying no one. Besides, this girl approves and who knows, I have a better chance of getting this girl with $2 million in my bank account.*

He pedals faster and arrives at his apartment in no time. He drops his bike and races up to his apartment. The door flies open startling his flatmate. Hershel quickly grabs the Staff and the towel it's wrapped in before placing it inside an umbrella cover. He inserts the umbrella cover along the side of his backpack and runs back out the door.

His flatmate opens his mouth to talk but Hershel is in and out in seconds.

At the front of his apartment building Hershel notices Emily sitting in the SUV with the windows rolled down.

"I'll race you," he shouts at Emily who shakes her head and smiles. Another gesture from Hershel that reminds her of Forrest Gump. She does find his quirkiness, energy and enthusiasm somewhat alluring.

Hershel is back at the café within 10 minutes huffing and puffing with the umbrella cover in his hand. Emily arrives at the café not long after.

"I beat you," Hershel smiles at Emily as the pair make their way inside the café to Goldberg's table. Hershel calmly sits down and removes the umbrella cover from its holder on the side of the backpack and hands it to Goldberg. Emily remains standing intrigued by the potential contents. She has read the old pocket Bible and accompanying notes several times and wants to know if this really is the Staff of Moses. Goldberg opens it, unwraps the towel and confirms it's there. He stops uncovering the Staff and looks up to smile at Emily. Goldberg motions over to Wells to bring the briefcase. Goldberg asks Emily to sit down as Wells arrives at the table and hands Goldberg the briefcase. He opens it and shows Hershel the money. It's all there. Goldberg quickly closes the briefcase and hands it to Hershel. Both men look at each other and smile.

An emotional Goldberg unwraps the towel and stares at the simple stick in his hand. He is in awe of its age, the smell of old timber, the petrified hard texture. His eyes light up as he notices the amber. Goldberg then looks at Wells then rubs four fingers across the top of his right ear. Wells nods, he knows that sign. The four fingers stand for the letter F and ear forming the word FEAR. Unbeknownst to anyone, Goldberg has just informed Wells that Hershel is a threat and ordered he be removed from the equation. Hershel's life is now in danger.

Goldberg carefully wraps the Staff with the towel sweeping his hands across the length of the Staff consumed by what he possesses, not once lifting his head.

"Tell me Hershel, apart from you who else knows about the Staff? Your brothers, sisters, your parents perhaps?" Goldberg asks.

Hershel shakes his head.

"No, just me...oh and an old rabbi here in New York who knows a lot more about it than I do," Hershel replies innocently.

Goldberg stops and looks up at Hershel.

"I would, well the UN that is, would certainly want to know more about the Staff. Do you have the old rabbi's details?" Goldberg asks politely.

Hershel doesn't hesitate and scrolls through his cell phone before giving Goldberg the location of Rabbi

Manassah's synagogue. Goldberg again looks at Wells and rubs his four fingers across the top of his right ear. Again, Wells nods. The message is received loud and clear, the old rabbi must go too. Goldberg asks Hershel if all the money is there. Hershel nods and Goldberg stands to leave with his coffee untouched. Goldberg is in full control and promptly ends the meeting before thanking Hershel in an attempt to provide some peace of mind.

"It's a very good thing you've done today. You may have just made the world a better place." He genuinely thanks Hershel who also stands and the men shake hands. Goldberg motions to Emily and Wells to depart. Emily follows protocol and shakes Hershel's hand and finally speaks to Hershel.

"Thank you, Hershel, and good luck. Call me sometime. We'll catch up just the two of us hey?" Emily smiles at Hershel before she motions to the remaining security staff to leave and makes sure she is the last one out of the café.

Hershel sits back down and stays at the table stunned by what has just occurred. It all happened so fast. As Emily walks away Hershel can't help but glance at her curvy rear and his face lights up with a huge smile. Hershel now knows that Emily's request to meet again will definitely be their first date. As Hershel stares, Emily turns around catching Hershel's eyes focused on her butt. Emily smiles and waves goodbye. An embarrassed Hershel quickly looks away. He got caught.

Little does Hershel know that Emily is seething at Goldberg. She was never told about the cash offer and also had no idea Goldberg confided in Mark Wells, who she despises given his creepy reputation in the UN.

Hershel motions to a waitress to come over and orders a celebratory meal, the biggest New York Rueben sandwich on the menu, with pickles on the side. His smile widens, he has money and an interested girl. Life is certainly good right now. He lets out a sigh of satisfaction. There are no regrets.

6

The custodians

The next morning a thunderstorm hovers over New York City. Hershel lays awake in his apartment, he hasn't slept at all. It didn't take long for the guilt of selling the Staff, failing to keep his promise to his grandfather and ignoring the old rabbi's warning to engulf his thoughts. Has he failed them and was that worth $2 million?

Hershel stares down at the briefcase next to the desk where the Staff once rested and ponders how he is going to deposit the money into his account without myriad questions from bank officers and attracting unwanted attention from the government? He doesn't understand why the transaction was in cash instead of the UN wiring such a large amount of money into his account; it would have been easier. Hershel questions whether what occurred was a Goldberg family or UN transaction. Regardless, the cash transaction is untraceable. So many questions and now even the money is a problem.

Hershel gets out of bed and makes his way into the kitchen. He notices a sticky Post-it Note on the fridge from his flatmate which reads 'Running late, borrowed your bike, thanks'. Hershel scrunches up the little paper, he doesn't need his bike, he has no intention of attending college today anyway. In the background, a television is running news on the hour. Amongst the stories a hit and run outside a New York synagogue which has killed an old rabbi. Hershel isn't paying attention. His head is buried in the fridge. He lifts his head and mumbles to himself, *Why am I looking for breakfast. I don't eat breakfast and besides I can just buy breakfast, every day in fact?*

While getting himself ready for the day a hot shower provides a moment of clarity. He needs to clear his conscience and decides he must visit the old rabbi to tell him about Goldberg's father and their amazing but slightly different Gaza story.

Hershel gets dressed and catches a bus downtown. He walks into a deli to have brunch and contemplates what his grandfather would be thinking if he was alive. Shapiro served with Goldberg's father but how well did they know each other? Did Goldberg's father really find the Staff first? Why has this part of the story only come out now? He quickly finishes his food and coffee and gets on the bus to make his way to see the old rabbi. As the bus gets closer to the synagogue, Hershel notices a single police car parked across the road in front of a deli. Nothing unusual for New York. Hershel steps off the bus and sees that police tape has cordoned off the area and a police officer taking photos of the ground. Hershel can't stop staring for some reason. He makes his way to the front of the synagogue and knocks on the door turning his head, still transfixed on the police car parked opposite.

A young rabbi opens the door, and speaks softly. "Hello Hershel, please take a seat, someone will be with you shortly."

Hershel sits down on a bench and thanks the young rabbi who walks away. Hershel has never met this young rabbi and is puzzled that he called Hershel by name. Hershel immediately notices that there are many people in the synagogue foyer scurrying around and not just rabbis. Something is wrong.

Before long a senior rabbi greets Hershel again by name. With a sad and somber stare, the senior rabbi sits down and places his hand on Hershel's shoulder,

"I know why you are here. It's a very sad day for us," he solemnly states as the senior rabbi's other hand holds Hershel's wrist.

Hershel is unaware and the senior rabbi senses the look of confusion on Hershel's face. The senior rabbi, makes the connection.

"Hershel, do you know what's happened?"

Hershel shakes his head. The senior rabbi puts his arm around Hershel and softly breaks the news.

"Rabbi Manassah, who you probably came to see today was accidentally killed last night by a hit and run driver just across the road outside the synagogue. It's very sad."

Hershel slumps back on the bench in disbelief. The senior rabbi looks around the foyer as people begin to stare at Hershel. He asks Hershel to follow him to his office away from the crowd. Hershel follows as the pair enter the senior rabbi's office. Hershel notices a young suited man standing next to the rabbi's desk. Hershel frowns as he enters the office and hesitates for a moment. The senior rabbi assures him everything is okay. Hershel enters and sits as the senior rabbi makes his way to sit behind his desk.

"I have been wanting to meet you for some time. Why did you come here today? Does it have anything to do with the meeting you had with Rabbi Manassah?" The senior rabbi asks concerned.

"Do you know about that?" Hershel nervously responds.

The senior rabbi nods.

"You mean the fact you possess part of the Staff of Moses? Yes, we all know about that," he says as he points with an open palm to the young suited man still standing next to the desk.

Hershel is astounded.

"We also know you sold out, sorry sold It to Isaac Goldberg of the United Nations yesterday for $2 million," the senior rabbi informs Hershel in a disappointed tone forcing Hershel to stand abruptly.

"How could you know that? Who are you guys? Who is this guy?" Hershel belts out the questions while pointing to the suited man.

The senior rabbi asks Hershel to sit and forgives such a temper.

"Come on Hershel, you have a meeting in a Jewish café in New York with Isaac Goldberg and you think people won't talk?" The senior rabbi smiles shrugging his shoulders and throwing his hands in the air.

Hershel admits he may be a little naive and composes himself before sitting back down as the senior rabbi continues.

"Hershel, let me tell you what happened after you met with Rabbi Manassah."

Hershel's begins to worry, he told Goldberg no one else knew about the Staff but more people know now. Hershel focuses his attention on the senior rabbi who is explaining his position and that of the synagogue.

"After your meeting, Rabbi Manassah returned to the synagogue and called a meeting with me. He told me that he believed you were in possession of the Staff and were well aware of the power it contains."

Hershel's hands rub his face nervously as the senior rabbi continues.

"We then contacted the Shin Bet for help. Do you know about Shin Bet Hershel?" the senior rabbi asks.

Hershel shakes his head. The senior rabbi again uses his open palm to point to the suited man who decides to introduce himself and his role.

"Hershel, have you heard of Israeli security agencies?" the suited man says getting straight to the point.

Hershel nods instantly and begins to sway slightly in his chair before responding in a shaky voice, "Mossad, you mean Mossad?"

The senior rabbi again uses both palms to calm Hershel down. The suited man continues.

"No, not Mossad Hershel, there are three security agencies of Israel, you know Mossad, that is foreign intelligence, Aman which is military intelligence and then there is internal security, the Shabak or the Shin Bet as we are known."

The suited man pauses as he rests his fingers on his chest to confirm his identity.

Hershel shakes his head not having any idea of the existence of Shin Bet.

The suited man elaborates.

"Do you know the motto of Shin Bet?" he asks as Hershel shakes his head,

"It is 'Defender that shall not be seen'. That is the literal meaning in Hebrew, though we prefer the phrase 'The unseen shield'," the suited man explains in a slow and soft voice so as to not alarm Hershel any further.

The senior rabbi tells Hershel that the suited man and others have been protecting all the rabbis in the synagogue since the incident this morning. They are also protecting Hershel and are aware the Staff was sold to Goldberg.

"Am I in any danger?" Hershel asks, acknowledging the severity of events.

The senior rabbi looks seriously at Hershel and tells him the truth.

"The old rabbi was in perfect health Hershel; he was old but in good shape. He walked across that road to that deli a thousand times. We spoke to several people on the street who observed a black SUV deliberately cross the wrong side of the road."

The senior rabbi tells Hershel the full story and Hershel again stands and begins to pace the room.

"Well, there is certainly a lot of shit going down right now, pardon me rabbi, and I've got a few things to do. I need to go back to my apartment."

Hershel shakes the rabbi's hand and gives the suited man a nod in appreciation of his protection. As Hershel makes his way outside the synagogue and across the street to catch the next bus, the senior rabbi and suited man watch through the office window.

"Watch over him even more closely now, others will be watching Mr Goldberg," the senior rabbi instructs the suited man.

Hershel paces along the bus stop all the while nervously looking over his shoulder. While on the bus he is judging the passengers, pedestrians and cars going by. He was already bothered and nervous and now he is paranoid. He moves seats making his way to the back of the bus and sits by a window. He begins to scrutinise people around him even more. The bus stops, a man outside knocks at Hershel's window telling him to hold the bus. It causes Hershel to jump out of his skin. As the bus takes off Hershel simply stares at the man who is screaming obscenities at Hershel for doing nothing to stop the bus. Hershel has zoned out.

At every bus stop he studies shop owners and pedestrians who are looking up at his face at the bus window – as most people do but for Hershel it is so noticeable it disturbs him. Each stare brings more and more worry and anxiety. As the bus approaches his stop, Hershel notices an ambulance and police car at the front of his apartment building. Hershel gets off the bus and slowly walks towards his apartment. The walk quickly turns from slow to a steady jog before Hershel begins to run to the scene. He is stopped from going any further by a policeman.

There in the gutter Hershel sees his mangled bicycle. Lying on the road, his flatmate. Paramedics are performing CPR before they place his flatmate on a gurney and into the ambulance. They are still working on reviving him when Hershel sees them stop and place a blanket over his flatmate's body. The ambulance doors close.

Hershel looks around paranoid. He hears witnesses telling the police the cyclist was run off the road by a black SUV. Hershel wastes no time and turns to grab the attention of the nearest policeman.

"Sir, officer sir?" Hershel pleads and the officer turns and listens.

"That's my bicycle sir and he was my flatmate. If you want to come upstairs with me, I will give you his parents' details."

Hershel is clearly upset as he informs the officer.

The officer obliges and informs a senior detective that he will accompany Hershel up to the apartment.

As they enter, the place is a little messy and the officer waits by the door. Hershel makes his way to his room and starts stuffing clothes into his backpack and grabs the briefcase.

"Ah, how long did you guys know each other? Did you know his family at all?" the officer asks loudly so Hershel can hear from his room.

"He was from Chicago and we were going to college together," Hershel yells back while he continues to pack belongings into his backpack.

The officer nods as Hershel appears in the kitchen ready to leave. He heads to the fridge and pulls off a small card handing it to the officer.

"Here, these are his parents' contact details and here is my card. I have an appointment to get to. You know my number if you have any questions. If you want to look around just close the door behind you, it locks itself," Hershel states hurriedly.

The officer nods his head and looks around before leaving with Hershel.

On the street, at the front of the apartment, Hershel cautiously looks around for any suspicious people or cars then makes his way onto the bus and heads for the synagogue. The bus ride is torturous, so much so Hershel ends up hiding his head between his knees not wanting to look at anything or anyone anymore. Before long he arrives at the synagogue and immediately notices two security guards at the front door. As Hershel approaches the two guards nod and open the synagogue door. Hershel is well known now and doesn't even need to knock. The senior rabbi greets him at the door and ushers him inside.

"I need to stay here for a little while," Hershel asks, flustered.

The senior rabbi nods as the men walk towards his office.

"My flatmate is dead, he was riding my bicycle and got hit by a car. I can't go to my parents. I can't involve them. I couldn't turn to anyone else."

Hershel breaks down, devastated by the events of the last few days and his irresponsibility.

The senior rabbi says nothing as they enter his office and sit down. A lady offers them coffee. Both men nod and say thank you. The senior rabbi comforts Hershel who is finding it hard to compose himself. His anxiety has caught up with him. The senior rabbi informs Hershel that he is welcome to stay at the *shul*, a type of community centre next to the synagogue used by the congregation to study or just get together. The senior rabbi insists Hershel stay for as long as he wants and that there are three bedrooms used by visiting rabbis. They are not very big rooms but they are safe and it will allow Hershel to keep a low profile for a little while.

"I am happy to pay my way," Hershel tells the senior rabbi between tears.

The senior rabbi notices the briefcase under Hershel's arm.

"You will be our guest here Hershel," the senior rabbi reassures him.

There is a knock on the door and the suited man enters followed by the lady with a tray of coffee and biscuits. She places the tray on the desk, smiles and leaves the office. As Hershel composes himself and places milk and a sugar into his coffee the senior rabbi asks him if he is a little calmer now. Hershel confirms he is feeling a little better.

The senior rabbi decides it's time to brief Hershel.

"You know Hershel, I think you should know everything."

Hershel stops sipping his coffee and places it on the desk.

"Rabbi Manassah explained to me all the things he mentioned to you in the library, yes. He also confirmed to us that you had part of the Staff and showed us the photos he took and some measurements he wrote down. It is then we decided to contact the Shin Bet and that's the reason why they are here.

"Hershel what most people do not know is that the Shin Bet were given the responsibility of locating, keeping and guarding Jewish artefacts. The keepers of every divine instrument of our faith."

The senior rabbi holds Hershel's wrist as a gesture of comfort as well as a plea to place some trust in him. The senior rabbi discloses more as he points to the suited man.

"This man is committed to Shin Bet; he may even know where the Ark of the Covenant is. Do you know about the Ark of the Covenant?" the senior rabbi quizzes Hershel.

"Of course, I know it," Hershel replies assuring the senior rabbi of his faith.

"You don't have that too, do you?" the senior rabbi quick-wittedly asks Hershel in an effort to lighten the mood.

Hershel doesn't smile and responds, "Everyone knows what it is rabbi, it was in Raiders with Harrison Ford. But I know nothing about the Shin Bet. Mossad and Aman yes. My parents are Jewish but not orthodox or traditional. We always referred to ourselves as casual Hebrews."

"Hershel, the most important responsibility of the Shin Bet is that they ensure the divine powers of all artefacts, the artefacts of our people, like the Staff, are upheld and not abused by anyone, and of utmost importance, that they don't fall into the wrong hands," the senior rabbi informs Hershel.

Hershel finally stands and delivers a warm handshake to the suited man again grateful for his role as custodian, defender and protector. The senior rabbi stands and asks Hershel to walk with him to another room. The suited man leads Hershel and the senior rabbi down the hallway. The senior rabbi explains to Hershel that until Shapiro found the black stick, no one knew where the Staff of Moses was located. There were too many claims of its existence and by different countries. He tells Hershel that the excitement amongst the rabbis and the Shin Bet after he met with Rabbi Manassah spurred many people into action.

The suited man stops at a door and produces a set of keys before unlocking the door. He walks in ahead of Hershel and the senior rabbi and begins turning on lights. The senior rabbi invites Hershel to enter and follows him into the room. Hershel immediately notices a well-lit display cabinet in the far corner of the small room. The senior rabbi walks Hershel to the corner. Before the men is a purple velvet-lined cabinet some six feet long containing six dark wooden sticks. The senior rabbi explains that the six sticks are imitations of the Staff and were manufactured by the Shin Bet from the limited knowledge gained from the notes and pictures Rabbi Manassah took when he met Hershel. Amazed, Hershel asks the senior rabbi if he can open the cabinet in order to study each of the imitations.

Hershel, picks up the first imitation.

"This one is too long," he tells the senior rabbi handing the imitation to the suited man. He picks up another.

"And this one is not heavy enough."

Hershel points to another imitation and lets the men know that it's not black enough and then at another that isn't quite thick enough. Hershel pulls out his cell phone and shows the suited man and the Senior Rabbi hundreds of photos of the Staff from every angle.

"Perhaps you can use these images to make an actual clone? You know I've held it so I know its weight and colour and stuff. Perhaps you can, you know make an unmistakable copy of the Staff instead of these…well, these best guesses."

The senior rabbi looks closely at the pictures as the suited man thanks Hershel for the images. Hershel then places his backpack on the floor and removes a small notebook.

"I made notes too. Here are my measurements, including the width of the Staff, its weight and length, the exact location of the amber and its size. I even drew the Staff to scale." Hershel shows the men as he unfolds a multi-page, life-size sketch of the Staff.

"These are things that were unknown until now," the senior rabbi exclaims.

Hershel continues.

"Remember rabbi, I had the Staff long enough and recorded everything about it."

The senior rabbi looks at the suited man who is flicking through Hershel's notebook amazed by all the information, and let's Hershel know.

"Wow, Hershel, this is fantastic. The details are perfect."

The senior rabbi asks the suited man whether they could reform the team and commence work on a clone straight away. The suited man nods his head.

"Get some rest now my son," the senior rabbi says as he smiles proudly at Hershel who nods his head and returns the smile. Thoughts that he has finally done some good cross his mind. Not enough to compensate for his actions to date but it's something.

7

Possession is obsession

Isaac Goldberg is at his lavish home, sitting by himself at the head of his elaborate dining table elated at his new acquisition. His eyes focus as they hover over an umbrella cover containing the Staff. He is finally alone and can take the time to examine his treasure thoroughly. He gently removes the Staff from the umbrella cover then unwraps the towel and is immediately in awe. An ancient and fragile object yet able to wield such unbelievable power, if his father's story is correct. As he continues to examine the Staff, each part he comes across makes him relive his father's story. Incredibly, his father's notes slowly come to life as they confirm each detail. Goldberg comes to the knot and the crystal his father spoke of which he realises is not crystal but amber. Goldberg is very careful not to press that area – he believes now that in fact the amber is the infamous trigger, the gateway for the damned.

Goldberg is more than intrigued and begins to understand why his father became so obsessed. He can't resist peering through the amber lifting the Staff to his right eye looking through it while keeping his left eye closed. He hears his wife calling him from the kitchen. He tells her he is in the dining room. As his wife enters the dining room Goldberg puts the Staff down but his wife notices.

"Is that a cane?" she asks puzzled at the object.

"Yes, yes, it is. It belongs to one of the representatives and he left it in my office," Goldberg responds quickly to divert any curiosity and further attention.

"Don't forget we have dinner with John and Sandra tonight," she politely reminds her husband as she walks away. Goldberg acknowledges the dinner commitment and his wife leaves the room. Goldberg takes another quick look through the amber and puts the Staff down. He pushes away from the dining room table and makes his way upstairs taking the Staff.

In the *en suite* of the master bedroom, Goldberg is at the wash basin preparing for dinner when he catches a glimpse of himself in the mirror and speculates whether he should shave or not. He turns and looks at the Staff perched on the bed and has an idea. If he looked through the amber, would he see his reflection in the mirror? For him, it would confirm that he is good, pure and will therefore be rewarded in the afterlife. Goldberg doesn't hesitate and walks back into the bedroom. He quickly gets dressed and takes the Staff into the bathroom. Again, he is in awe of the object and raises the Staff slightly before lowering it again. He looks at his reflection in the mirror. He's not ready to look, he could look, but should he look? What if he doesn't like what the Staff reveals? He wants to know but also needs to find out if the Staff works. He closes his eyes and slowly brings the Staff up to his head. He takes a deep breath and places the Staff in front of his face with eyes closed. He prepares to open his right eye to look through the amber.

"You finished yet Isaac?" Goldberg's wife asks annoyingly as she enters the bathroom at that moment, startling Goldberg and preventing him from looking through the amber.

Goldberg provides no intelligible answer, just nods his head and grunts as he walks past his wife and back out into the bedroom. As Goldberg gathers his socks and shoes, he sits on the bed concerned. How long was his wife standing behind him? This is the beginning of what will be an oversupply of paranoia, common for those who possess the Staff. Having missed his opportunity in front of the mirror Goldberg still needs to know. He leaves his socks and shoes and picks up the Staff and walks towards the bathroom where his wife is in the shower. Steam on the shower glass hides his presence as he looks at his wife and raises the Staff to his right eye. He looks all around for what seems an eternity but he sees nothing other than the steam covered shower glass. He looks again and realises his wife is not appearing on the other side. He brings the Staff back down, blinks to clear his eyes and raises the Staff to look again, desperately wanting to see that his wife is there on the other side and that she is good and pure. She is not. Goldberg lowers the Staff and his face is pale. At that moment his wife turns around and wipes the steam off the glass noticing Goldberg is standing in the bathroom.

"Isaac, you're in here? You look like you've seen a ghost, are you okay?"

Goldberg nods and slowly makes his way back to the bedroom. He sits at the edge of the bed and his shoulders slump before releasing a tear. The Staff's power is that it discriminates, it doesn't lie, his wife is damned. He returns the Staff to its covers and places his hands across its length. He asks why. Why his wife? What did she do? Goldberg needs to know.

In a fashionable New York restaurant, the Goldbergs are at dinner with their friends. Goldberg is present though his mind is far removed from conversation and he finds it difficult to engage with his friends. He studies his wife all night hoping to find a clue as to why. He manages a wry smile every time his wife catches him staring at her. His friends notice and attempt to engage in conversation. Goldberg is disconnected.

At breakfast the next morning Goldberg is untalkative. He has been awake for hours. His wife enters the kitchen.

"You were a bundle of joy last night," she says sarcastically.

Goldberg grabs his car keys.

"I'll be out for an hour or so," he replies as he leaves the house.

In his car, his father's notes haunt him. *Those that do not appear through the Staff die as soon as you press the crystal.*

Goldberg smacks his hand on the steering wheel in disbelief. Why his wife? She has been a wonderful mother and supporter through his entire political career. She comes from a very wealthy and respected Jewish family with an impeccable track record in her own right, fighting for human rights. What could his wife have done that has condemned her in the afterlife? Is it something in her past or present life? Goldberg continues to question himself the entire journey from his home to the UN building.

Arriving in the UN garage, Goldberg hurriedly makes his way to his office where he sits at his desk and buries his head in his hands. He simply can't believe his wife is doomed. Before their marriage, given the importance of his political standing and promising future, his wife agreed to be subject to an investigation into her background and family life. Despite every aspect of her life being scrutinised the assessment showed nothing that could jeopardise Goldberg's career. Whatever has caused the condemnation has happened after they were married.

Goldberg picks up the phone and tells Head of UN Security Mark Wells to come to his office to discuss security protocols.

Before long Wells arrives at Goldberg's office. He makes his way to his friend and both men embrace. Goldberg closes the door and both men sit on the lounges. The men exchange standard pleasantries before Goldberg explains that there may be a security issue at his home and that he would like the phones tapped and CCTV installed if possible. Goldberg advises he is happy to sign whatever documentation is necessary to grant permission and stresses the urgency and secrecy of the job. Wells is happy to comply and wastes no time. He promises to immediately brief a security crew and dispatch an installation team to Goldberg's home tomorrow morning.

Later that day Goldberg facilitates yet another dysfunctional meeting of the UN Council for Religious Coexistence. This time he has no energy to challenge the unacceptable behaviour and the meeting is chaotic. Now desperate, having exhausted all avenues of making the representatives work together, Goldberg sits in his chair slumped and the entire assembly and Emily notices the disengaged body language. Emily makes her way to the chair pretending Goldberg has called her over.

"Are you okay, do you need a coffee or water refill?" she asks quietly.

"Just tired, sick and tired if you know what I mean?" he replies in a croaky and frustrated voice.

Emily sees the toll the under-secretary-general role is taking on Goldberg. The meeting ends early and Emily escorts Goldberg to his office. She suggests he head home offering to complete the council meeting minutes, media notice and prepare the agenda for the next meeting. It's late, Goldberg agrees and thanks Emily before making his way home.

As Goldberg enters his home, he makes his way towards the kitchen but stops short of entering. He senses his wife at the kitchen bench. She is there. In front of her, again, another bottle, half empty and her glass full.

"You took off in a hurry this morning," she giggles loudly and half-drunk, struggling to get the words out and not once looking at her husband.

Goldberg looks around angrily, there is no dinner. He doesn't enter the kitchen preferring the solace of his study. He contemplates what his wife could have done. His mind flashes back to their time together before they had children and the wonderful times they shared. His mind looks for a blemish in their relationship. Despite his efforts and several hours in thought he comes up empty. She has been a good wife and mother. His wife appears at the study doorway.

"It's very late, you coming to bed?" she manages to ask as her body sways.

Goldberg doesn't even look up. He can't look her in the eye.

"If you can remember, there is a UN security team coming here early tomorrow morning to make sure this house meets the new UN security standards for the homes of under-secretaries," Goldberg states. He is lying and politely fakes a smile before looking at his wife and saying goodnight. His wife nods and leaves.

The next morning Goldberg wakes up alone. He has slept in from what was a restless night. He makes his way downstairs and walks into the kitchen to find his wife having breakfast. He notices two UN security officers installing a camera but the men are looking at his wife and whispering. His wife has her dressing gown slightly open and a little more than just cleavage is on display. Goldberg politely motions to his wife to keep her dressing gown closed.

"These guys aren't eunuchs," Goldberg whispers to her shaking his head.

His wife does what she's told, pretending it was an accident. There is no conversation at breakfast. Goldberg's head is buried in a newspaper and his wife is on her iPad either on social media or sending emails and messages to her friends.

As they finish breakfast the UN security officers confirm they have completed the job. Mrs Goldberg gives them a teasing wave goodbye.

"I have nothing on until this afternoon so will be heading off after lunch," Goldberg informs his wife sharply.

She nods, no words are spoken as she makes her way upstairs.

Goldberg stays downstairs and makes his way into his study. He sits at the desk and stares blankly into space. He notices his father's notes in the drawer. He carefully removes them and begins reviewing them. He goes over them again and again. This time he is looking for any information from meetings with rabbis on whether the condemnation verdict by the Staff is reversible in some way. He frantically searches but there is nothing.

Around lunchtime, with no sign of his wife, Goldberg leaves to return to the UN building. He makes his way into his office and abruptly leaves his briefcase and turns around.

"Just going downstairs. Be back soon," he tells Emily, as he makes his way to the elevators before getting in.

Goldberg enters the security floor and monitoring centre where he is welcomed by UN officers. He asks to listen to anything that might be happening at his home. The security officer begins telling Goldberg about the purpose and abuse of such security devices. Goldberg confirms his understanding. The security crew hand him headphones and he begins to listen intently. Goldberg hears a live telephone conversation and tells the crew to be quiet. They all put on headphones. The conversation is between Mrs Goldberg and her mother. It is very personal as Mrs Goldberg is disclosing that despite her love for him, she feels her and Isaac have grown apart as a couple. Goldberg takes the headphones off and in a moment of clarity questions whether what he is doing is morally right. If anything, the trust his wife had for him has been breached. The headphones stay off. A guilt filled Goldberg walks out of the security office and thanks the security crew.

Before long Goldberg appears at Emily's desk. She looks up and notices an unfamiliar expression on his face.

"Is everything okay, you look disappointed and worried?" she asks caringly.

"I'm fine, fine. Come into the office and we'll go through yesterday's things," Goldberg responds in a pedestrian manner.

Emily follows Goldberg into his office who sits at his desk and takes a deep breath as Emily begins to hand over a copy of the minutes of yesterday's UN Council meeting together with the agenda for the next meeting. Goldberg takes time to read the minutes and agenda in an attempt to put his concerns about his wife aside for a moment. The two are in deep discussion and take over two hours to review and amend the UN documentation before they are interrupted by a knock on the door. A security officer walks in.

"Sir, may I speak with you please?" he asks in a deep serious tone.

Goldberg asks Emily to return to her desk. He follows the security guard out of the office to the elevators. The two men are quiet as they make their way back to the security floor's monitoring centre. The security guard holds the door open for Goldberg who enters the room. He immediately notices the CCTV installed that morning in his home is relaying live images. Goldberg watches as he is handed a pair of headphones which he puts on subconsciously. Goldberg can clearly see and hear that his wife is entertaining a young man in their living room. The man seems very comfortable helping himself to the liquor cabinet. It's clearly not his first visit. As the man walks to the kitchen Goldberg asks security to switch cameras and zoom in on the man's face. Despite the clarity Goldberg doesn't recognise him. The camera then follows the man back to the living room. There on the large monitor in front of Goldberg and the entire security crew on duty, is a scantily clad Mrs Goldberg lying on a leather lounge. The unknown man then appears on the same monitor. He places his drink on the coffee table and lies on top of her.

"I've seen enough," Goldberg tells the security team as he rips his headphones off and commands the cameras be turned off. The security team do as they're told. Goldberg is hiding his shock and dismay very well. He knows his wife is not in any danger so this is not a security issue. The security team leave the room.

Mark Wells arrives at the monitoring centre.

"I came over as soon as I heard," he informs Goldberg before escorting him out of the room to the elevators.

"Isaac, this is a private matter and my men are sworn to keep all matters confidential," he reassures Goldberg. "I've helped you before my friend. What would you like us to do from here?" Wells' statements are proof of his loyalty and friendship.

As the elevator opens Goldberg places his hand on his friend's shoulder and cracks a small smile.

"Nothing my friend, this is my issue, my problem," Goldberg informs Wells as he walks into the waiting elevator and gives Wells a small weak semi-salute goodbye.

As the elevator doors close Goldberg breaks down in tears. As he approaches his office floor, he begins to wipe his face in an attempt to compose himself. His mood soon turns to anger. Goldberg storms past Emily's desk and into his office slamming the door closed.

Emily looks around at the other administrative staff and makes her way to Goldberg's office putting her ear against the closed door. She hears Goldberg swearing and throwing things around the office. She hears a glass break and is startled. Goldberg yells out for Emily. Scared, she takes a deep breath and pauses stepping up and down on the spot to make it seem as though she is making her way to the door despite the fact she is already there.

She enters the room and is berated about her commitment to the UN which is followed by a list of tasks for her to undertake urgently. Emily is always ahead of deadlines; she has never seen Goldberg lose his temper or get angry even during the most heated UN Council meetings. He informs her that he will not be in tomorrow and expects her to deliver the requested work.

Goldberg collects his things and hurriedly leaves the office for home. The drive provides an opportunity to clear his mind and think things through. Where did his marriage go wrong, he wonders? When did she fall out of love? As he nears home it dawns on him. The Staff speaks the truth and he realises it is adultery that's condemned his wife. Goldberg begins to break down, he is devastated, it's all too much and the strain of keeping his emotions in check throughout the day's events are now released. A few minutes later his cell phone rings. It's his wife.

"Isaac, Isaac you need to come home. Your father has had a fall and your mother has taken him to the hospital," his wife says worriedly.

"Which hospital?"

He waits.

"Okay, I am going straight there." Goldberg's response is cold, ice cold.

The thought of his wife's infidelity and now his father's emergency causes a lack of concentration and the car jumps the curb causing Goldberg to jar his right foot trapping his ankle underneath the accelerator pedal. He puts his left foot on the brake and the car comes to a screeching and shuddering stop inches from a tree. He puts the handbrake on and puts the car in park. He closes his eyes and takes a deep breath as smoke from his brakes and tyres surround the car. As people approach to see if he is alright, Goldberg composes himself and continues on his way to the hospital.

In a dimly lit hospital room, a limping Goldberg greets his mother.

"Isaac, he is not good, he has hurt his head and they want him to sleep." His mother is in tears and stammers through her words.

Goldberg hugs his mother and walks over to be beside his father. He places a hand on his father's shoulder. The day's events see Goldberg show no emotion. He cannot feel anymore. A dysfunctional council, a cheating wife and now his father on his death bed. Goldberg is on the verge of madness. His mother senses her son's pain and walks over to stand next to him. She embraces her son and cries. Much like his father, Goldberg remains motionless.

8

Emily's concern

It's early Friday morning at the UN offices and Emily is sitting at her desk. She is alone having arrived much earlier than the other assistants. She has plenty to do and begins by reading her emails. She notices an email from Goldberg informing her of his father's fall as well as reminding Emily of the work Goldberg has asked her to do. It ends with Goldberg reminding Emily that he will not be in for the day and has decided to take the coming week off due to his father's condition. Emily is an exceptional staff member, and her unprofessional treatment by Goldberg is totally undeserved and unacceptable but she is strong.

Emily closes the email and rests her eyes. A thousand questions run through Emily's mind concerning Goldberg. What was the security officer visit all about? Why was Goldberg furious immediately after he returned from the security floor? Does he see the lack of progress caused by the dysfunctional Council for

Religious Coexistence as a personal failure? What about his inability to influence and persuade individual members, has that finally got to him? Have there been threats by member nations? Is it all too much and does he feel helpless that everything threatens to derail his professional career?

Emily continues to ask questions and look for more causes. What is she forgetting? What has changed Goldberg apart from UN matters and his father's recent illness? Frustrated she has no answers and tries to start on the workload she has been given. As she collects her papers, she glances across her desk and catches a glimpse of Hershel Rosen's home-made business card. Emily smiles then makes the connection. Is Goldberg's frailty the result of his taking possession of the Staff of Moses?

Emily finds it hard to concentrate. She is genuinely concerned for Goldberg and his destructive mood change, and her mind is consumed by these unanswered questions. Emily is diligent and decides to investigate starting with Goldberg's office. She leaves her desk to walk the short distance across the hallway. She stops and looks down each end of the hallway to make sure she isn't seen by anyone else. She enters the office quietly closing the door behind her and, almost as if she were on tip-toes, quickly makes her way to Goldberg's desk. She sits to compose herself, not knowing where to begin. She starts with the obvious by shuffling the papers on the desk. She picks up a page then another and begins to read but stops. She knows this desk like the back of her hand, she organises everything on it, it's her system. There is nothing there. Emily turns to Goldberg's personal laptop which he has strangely left behind. Without hesitation she enters his login and password. Unsure what she is looking for she starts going through his UN network related files first. There is nothing on that network that she isn't already aware of. She then looks through the contents of a personal drive and files on the laptop which is separate to the UN network but again there is nothing of importance. She then notices that Goldberg's personal email is still signed in. Emily pauses. She contemplates her next action. Emily is not one to break protocol and hesitates looking up at the closed office door. She could easily go through the emails, but should she? She could save his career. With a burning desire to know what it is that's causing Goldberg's behaviour, she browses the email folders. Armed with a noble motive Emily begins to go through each folder and comes across one called 'Staff' with a capital S.

Suddenly there's a knock on the door. A deep voice calls.

"Isaac, Isaac, can I come in." It's Mark Wells, Head of UN Security.

Emily looks up startled. She knows that voice and starts quitting every program before simply closing the laptop.

"Just a minute," she responds and hurries to the door but doesn't get to open it. Wells has used his master key and lets himself in. Emily arrives at the door at the same time and the two find themselves uncomfortably face to face.

"Hello Mr Wells, you beat me to the door," she smiles, flustered and nervous.

Wells looks at Emily's eyes then looks around the room before returning to stare all over Emily's face. His eyes then shift and he creepily inspects Emily, looking up and down her body suspiciously.

"What are you doing in here?" Wells is direct and shows no emotion.

"Mr Goldberg is not in today and left me a huge list of things to do. He lets me work in here sometimes because it's quiet. Too much traffic out there to concentrate," Emily replies very composed.

She points to her desk and smiles again hoping she doesn't sound too phony realising she is trying to appear calm in front of the Head of UN Security. Wells doesn't engage, preferring to talk down to the young assistant.

"I'll call him on his cell phone then. If he calls please let him know I was looking for him," Wells commands.

Emily nods and relief appears on her face at the thought that their brief encounter is almost over. Wells keeps his eyes on Emily as he closes the door. Emily turns and leans against the door and breathes a sigh of relief.

"Creep," she whispers under her breath. She's never liked Wells. Maybe it's because as head of security he has to keep his distance from employees and always be impartial or rather suspicious; either way he just rubs Emily up the wrong way.

With Wells gone Emily returns to the laptop on the desk and contemplates whether to continue or not. She then questions why Wells needed to talk to Goldberg? She thinks for a second whether Wells knows something. She is now more intrigued than ever. Her confident handling of Wells gives her just enough courage to continue to explore the "Staff" folder and begins to scroll down. She notices the folder contains emails from Goldberg's father but also two emails from Wells' personal email address and they stand out due to the high cap headings. The first email has no body or text just a simple heading, it reads "RABBI MANASSAH" The second email again has no message or text, only a heading, "WRONG KID". There are no replies from Goldberg to Wells on these emails nor has anyone been copied in. The emails don't appear to be part of a conversation or email trail. Fearing this may all be a red herring she conducts one last investigation. She Googles 'Rabbi Manassah' and his profile appears. Emily then makes the connection remembering the name of the rabbi is the same as the one Hershel spoke about when the Staff was bought by Goldberg that day in the café. The next article sends chills up her spine. It's a *New York Post* piece on the hit and run death of the rabbi. She notices the date of the event. The day after the meeting in the café. She cross-references the news article with the email and notices it was sent the same day and only an hour or so after the Police estimation of the time of the accident. Emily starts closing down all programs and closes the laptop.

Frightened, she stands and looks up to stare out the window. One thought leads to another and another.

She asks herself whether the emails, and therefore Goldberg and Wells, have anything to do with the rabbi's death? Emily leaves everything on the desk and office just as she found it and walks out.

Emily returns to her desk across the hall. She is flustered and contemplates taking action but what can she do. Who can she ask or tell? How does she even begin to investigate the link between Goldberg, Wells and Rabbi Manassah's death? She really has nothing concrete that would warrant going to the police. She rests her head in her hands. Out of the corner of her eye she notices Mrs Rosen's file and again resting on top is Hershel's home-made business card. Emily pauses before realising that Hershel is someone, perhaps the only person, she could talk to.

Concerned with eavesdropping assistants, Emily stands and returns to the peace and quiet of Goldberg's office. She paces around the desk in two minds whether to call Hershel – after all, she did catch him staring at her behind when they last met so if she asks to meet him, there is little chance he will say no. Nothing to lose really. Emily sits at Goldberg's desk and calls Hershel.

Hershel is lying on his bed in the *shul* when his cell phone rings. He instantly recognises the number and nervously answers, "Ahh, hello."

"Hello, hello, Hershel? This is Emily," she whispers.

Excited to hear her voice Hershel sits straight up and like the true nerd that he is tries to act cool by straightening his clothes and brushing his hair with his fingers despite the fact Emily is not in the room and can't see him.

"Oh, hi, yeah, how are you?" His lack of experience in communicating with females goes unnoticed.

Emily informs him that she knows they haven't spoken in a while and that she would like to catch up with him. She finishes with, "Why didn't you call me?"

Hershel stands from his bed to check his hair in the mirror and says, "I was going to but things got a little crazy."

Emily dismisses the response and pushes on.

"How about a catch-up this afternoon, same café?" she confidently asks.

Hershel's response is lightning fast. "No...I mean let's meet somewhere else, okay?"

He provides Emily with the details of the deli across the road from the synagogue.

"Okay, this afternoon is perfect as the boss is away, see you then." Emily hangs up, and feels a little better now she has found someone to confide in. Hershel throws his cell phone on the bed and performs what can only be described as a nerdy victory dance. This is definitely a date now, no question about it.

Hershel picks out some trendy clothes and skips to the shower. He even shaves what little facial hair he has. He smells good and his hair looks perfect.

As he leaves the *shul*, he walks past the senior rabbi's office to let him know that Emily called and that he is catching up with her across the road. The senior rabbi nods and suggests Hershel bring along the suited man. The taste of normality Hershel was feeling is erased in an instant as he realises the reason he is staying at the *shul* and the protected life he is now leading. Hershel agrees with the senior rabbi's suggestion and leaves the synagogue with the suited man trailing behind.

Emily is already standing at the front of the deli when Hershel arrives. She makes a point of shaking his hand then draws him closer to embrace him. Hershel really hoped for a kiss hello but the embrace is wonderful. The suited man goes unnoticed sitting somewhere else in the deli. Emily grabs Hershel's hand and leads him to a table. Hershel smiles, now there is hand contact and that too doesn't go unnoticed. Hershel keeps smiling. The pair take off their jackets before sitting down. A waitress appears and takes their order before quickly walking away.

"Okay, so how have you been?" Emily excitedly begins.

"I've been okay, just relaxing," Hershel responds blandly.

Emily drops her shoulders and whispers, "It's been a little while since I've seen you. Tell me what have you bought, how have you used the money? Some nice things I'm sure?"

It is the furthest thing from Hershel's mind. In fact, he has spent less than $1000 and that was all on food and nice clothes.

"Oh, I'm trying to be smart with my money. Have to think about my future, you know," Hershel responds with an answer he thinks a girl wants to hear from a future boyfriend, and it works. Emily is impressed.

Before long, their coffees arrive and both nod to thank the waitress. Emily is done with the idle chit-chat and begins to tell Hershel what has happened to Goldberg, including his temper, his ill father and the lack of progress with the UN Council meetings.

"Look Hershel, I really need to ask you something?"

Hershel sits up straight and pays attention before frowning at Emily who continues.

"I have to ask you. Tell me, did possessing the Staff result in bad luck?"

Emily hangs on his response.

Hershel is sipping his coffee and shakes his head. He is love-struck and only hears part of Emily's update but feels obliged to respond.

"Well a few bad things *have* happened...Rabbi Manassah was killed," he informs Emily. She wants to interrupt but refrains as Hershel continues.

"The next day my flatmate was riding *my* bike and got knocked down and killed, so yeah there have been a few 'bad' events."

Emily gently places her hand over Hershel's on the table. Hershel is unsure how much to say but Emily's soft caring gesture gives him the comfort to open up.

"Actually Emily, if I was honest, those accidents have made me a nervous wreck. I am not going to college anymore, I'm not living in my apartment, I'm living at the *shul* in the synagogue. I haven't seen and can't even call or tell my parents about any of this including the $2 million because quite frankly, they'll freak out." Hershel is comfortable to tell her everything. Emily is sickened by Hershel's issues and he notices the change in her face. Hershel stops talking about his problems. He is clearly not on a date.

"Hey, are you okay?" Hershel whispers as he places his arm around Emily.

"I don't know what to do, what do I do?" she asks Hershel while crying on his shoulder. Clearly the last few days have taken their toll on her.

Hershel tells Emily he has been confiding in the senior rabbi and suggests they visit him. Emily is reluctant at first but when Hershel assures her that she needs someone to trust, and he trusts the senior rabbi, Emily agrees. The pair finish their coffees, Hershel pays, of course. As they walk out Hershel extends a hand to Emily and she takes it, wanting it as much as needing it. Emily looks into Hershel's eyes, she likes him.

Hershel now has a key to the *shul* and opens the door for Emily and leaves it open for the suited man to enter.

Hershel is still holding Emily's hand as they make their way to the senior rabbi's office. Hershel knocks on the door.

"Rabbi, are you free to talk?" he asks.

The senior rabbi opens the door and greets the pair with a smile.

"You must be Emily?" the senior rabbi says as he shakes Emily's hand.

Hershel notices the suited man assigned to protect him is following a few steps behind and he follows the pair into the room. Emily squeezes Hershel's hand to get his attention. She is uncertain about the identity of the suited man. The senior rabbi asks the couple to sit down as the suited man takes his usual position standing next to the desk. The senior rabbi addresses the pair.

"You both look troubled, what is it?" the rabbi asks as Hershel looks at Emily.

She hesitates and looks around the room to see if anyone else is coming in.

"Is he okay?" Emily asks of the suited man.

"Yes, he's good, he knows everything," the senior rabbi and Hershel respond in unison.

Emily takes a deep breath before introducing herself to the senior rabbi as Goldberg's assistant. She begins to disclose her concerns, specifically the dramatic changes in Goldberg's behaviour and that it all appears to coincide with his UN appointment, his father's accident and the purchase of the Staff from Hershel. The senior rabbi immediately dismisses the Staff as a cause explaining that there is nothing in the Bible nor in any teachings about the Staff that impacts a person's behaviour. Emily says nothing as the rabbi leans forward.

"But, knowing that you own the Staff and have its power at your disposal certainly will change people," he warns as he leans back in his chair.

The senior rabbi asks Emily if she knows of any other reason for Goldberg's temper other than the ones she has already mentioned. Emily shakes her head. The senior rabbi leans forward and smiles to calm Emily.

"So, it seems the fact Mr Goldberg has the weight of the world on his shoulders may have something to do with his temper and behaviour." He states bluntly.

"That's what I thought," Emily tells the senior rabbi, and leaning forward. continues. "There's more. I found two private emails to Goldberg from the Head of UN Security, Mark Wells. They both have a heading only. In capital letters one has the heading 'Rabbi Manassah' and the other has the heading 'Wrong Kid'."

The senior rabbi sits still in his chair, gently rubbing his chin.

"Tell me Emily," the suited man begins, "are you familiar with the types of vans and cars the UN uses?" Emily looks at the suited man and he explains further.

"You see here in New York the UN have black limousines, town cars and black SUVs and that's it. All other vehicles are military and belong to the peace-keeping forces, none of which are here in New York."

"Well yes, that's right," she happily confirms unsure about the line of questioning.

The senior rabbi's phone rings and he attempts to excuse himself. Hershel asks the senior rabbi if he and Emily can go for a walk and he agrees asking the pair to return to his office in 15-20 minutes and not later. As the couple leave the senior rabbi motions to the suited man to follow them.

Hershel seizes the opportunity to be alone with Emily and they walk around the block to Central Park. It's cold and Hershel grabs her hand.

"Everything is going to be okay," he reassures Emily. "The senior rabbi will sort things out. There are things happening in the background that you don't know about yet."

Emily smiles, enjoying the concern and interest Hershel is displaying. She changes the subject.

"You know, I wondered why you never called me," she tells Hershel.

Hershel is taken aback and lost for words.

"After all, I left you my business card, I really wanted you to call me."

It's the first real sign Hershel has had that Emily was actually interested in him. Given everything that happened only days after he last met Emily, the thought of calling her never really crossed his nerdy socially retarded mind.

"Well, I'm here now," Hershel replies tenderly while staring into Emily's eyes.

Hershel leans across and gives her a kiss on the forehead and hugs her.

Emily nestles her head on Hershel's chest. Love is certainly in the air. The couple continue walking arm in arm.

They walk for some time making small talk. They share a laugh here and there watching street performers in the park. After a while they decide to sit on a nearby bench. Hershel takes off his coat and places it around Emily's shoulders. There is no more conversation as Emily plants a soft kiss on Hershel's lips. He fumbles giving her a slightly harder kiss before the couple embrace. A bell rings on Hershel's cell phone. The message from the senior rabbi is simple; 'Return at once'. Hershel looks around to see the suited man already standing behind him waiting to escort the pair back to the synagogue.

The senior rabbi greets them at the door and steers the couple into his office. He begins to inform them that after further thought there is a real danger in Hershel and Emily even being seen together. There are also questions the senior rabbi would like to ask Emily in the morning and pleads with her to stay at the *shul* overnight. She agrees. The senior rabbi gives her a bathroom kit and towel and Emily and Hershel make their way to the *shul*. Emily asks Hershel if she can borrow a t-shirt and follows him to his room. Once in Hershel's room the couple embrace. Emily softly lands a kiss on Hershel's cheek.

"There, I have just paid you the overnight fee for the use of one of your t-shirts," she whispers. Hershel hands her a freshly cleaned and pressed t-shirt that was sitting on his bed. Emily grabs the t-shirt and heads for the door.

"Do you need any other clothes, same overnight fee?" Hershel offers.

As Emily gets to the doorway she stops and without looking back says, "Staring at my butt again Hershel?"

Hershel is embarrassed and mumbles goodnight as Emily leaves, walking down the hallway to her room. Hershel stands halfway between his doorway and the hall and smiles as Emily gives him a little wave.

"Good night." The suited man appears behind Hershel and responds to Emily's wave in a booming voice which startles Hershel. Emily enters her room and closes the door behind her.

"Hershel, the rabbi would like to talk to you," the suited man says as he leads Hershel back to the office.

The senior rabbi greets Hershel and asks him to sit down while the suited man remains standing next to the desk as always.

"My friend, we have been honest with you from the start and we need to keep being honest," the senior rabbi explains while the suited man nods and interjects.

"We have been investigating the death of both Rabbi Manassah and your flatmate. It seems both deaths were caused by a black SUV and that's the reason we asked Emily about the UN vehicles.

Hershel looks confused. The suited man continues.

"Until now we have not been able to prove it but Emily's email story has had us thinking. The email titled 'Rabbi Manassah' could be a message of confirmation, you know like 'mission accomplished' given the fact that it was sent so soon after the rabbi's death. But it's the second email that has us more concerned."

"You mean the one titled 'Wrong Kid'?" Hershel asks, well aware of the situation.

The suited man continues. "You see, all we have to go on is the email title. Your flatmate was riding your bike that day as he arrived at your apartment and was hit by a black SUV from behind."

Hershel fails to make the connection.

"They got the wrong kid, Hershel, your flatmate was the 'wrong kid'," the suited man spells out. "It was supposed to be you on that bike."

Heavy rain begins to pour on the synagogue roof as a loud clap of thunder and lightning illuminates the night. Hershel sits back in his chair speechless.

"Hershel, we think there is a possibility that in some way Goldberg is responsible for both incidents. He may have wanted to eliminate anyone connected to the Staff."

The senior rabbi calms the room by letting Hershel know that it is still an investigation and whilst this is a great lead, there is no proof yet. The senior rabbi reinforces the importance of Hershel staying at the *shul*. Hershel nods before getting up slowly to leave the room. He thanks the suited man and senior rabbi for everything they are doing for him.

As Hershel walks down the hall from the synagogue to the *shul* there is another clap of thunder overhead. He decides to visit Emily's room to make sure she is all right. He knocks on the door and Emily answers quickly. She has been pacing around her room unable to sleep. She invites Hershel in. The two sit on the edge of the bed and talk about the first time they met and the subsequent meeting with Goldberg including the race back to the café with the Staff. It helps ease the tension and both have a much-needed laugh. Emily says thank you to Hershel for everything he's done that day before reaching over to give him a peck on the cheek. As they hug and comfort each other Hershel makes his move. He looks deeply into Emily's eyes and draws her close. She surrenders and they both kiss passionately.

Early the next morning a knock on the door wakes Hershel and Emily. Hershel dresses quickly and gets to the door. Emily hides under the blanket. It's the coffee lady.

"Good morning, the rabbi would like to see you in his office please," she whispers softly.

Hershel nods and closes the door. He informs Emily to get ready as he gathers the rest of his clothes and returns to his room to shower and dress.

At the senior rabbi's office, the suited man is again discussing Emily's evidence from yesterday and briefing the senior rabbi on what he believes is happening with Goldberg. Hershel knocks on the door. The senior rabbi motions to the suited man to let Hershel in. As he opens the door, he notices Emily is with Hershel.

"Good morning my dear. Did you rest well?" the senior rabbi asks politely but doesn't wait for an answer.

"Would you mind having some breakfast in the kitchen as there is something we would like to discuss with Hershel privately?" The senior rabbi's request to Emily is said in-between smiles.

Hershel looks at Emily and lets her know he will meet her in the kitchen soon. The suited man closes the door and he and Hershel sit down at the desk opposite the senior rabbi.

The suited man begins. "Hershel, what we told you last night about the UN cars being connected to the murder of Rabbi Manassah and your flatmate seems more than just a possibility. We can prove it with Emily's help. Do you think she can be trusted?"

Hershel looks at the senior rabbi and answers immediately. "Um, yes, why not? She came to me, to us, for help. She is genuinely concerned and I believe that. Oh, you think Goldberg sent her? He doesn't even know she is here," Hershel assures the men.

The suited man looks at the senior rabbi as Hershel insists on including her in any course of action. The senior rabbi agrees with Hershel and motions to him to have breakfast with Emily and come back later. Hershel leaves the room. The senior rabbi and suited man begin to discuss Emily. The issue is not about trusting her, it's about getting her involved in any strategy to investigate the death of Rabbi Manassah and Hershel's flatmate. She is the closest UN person to Goldberg so a great asset, however, the key will be how covert she can be within the UN building and not exposing her to Goldberg and Wells who are, potentially, murderers.

Hershel joins Emily for breakfast. She reminds him it's Saturday morning and it would be nice to spend some time together.

"Okay, we'll see where the senior rabbi thinks it's safe for us to go," Hershel responds, realising the freedom he once had is no more, at least for the time being.

Emily understands the position they are both in and agrees. The couple finish breakfast and make their way to the senior rabbi's office.

Emily knocks on the door and enters the office cautiously.

"Is it okay to come in?" she asks.

The senior rabbi nods and asks her to sit with Hershel. The suited man stands next to the desk as always and wastes no time in briefing Emily on their theory about the emails and their relation to the death of Rabbi Manassah and Hershel's flatmate. He is adamant it was Hershel who was supposed to be killed that day and lets the couple know. Emily covers her mouth with one hand and extends her other hand to hold Hershel's. The suited man continues.

"The black SUV that struck Rabbi Manassah was seen driving off with no licence plates. Well at least no rear licence plate. It's quite hard to believe but the story the witness told police states the SUV's rear licence plate seemed to 'appear suddenly' much further down the street and by then it was too far away to make out any details."

Emily and Hershel look at each other and focus back on the suited man as he continues.

"Emily, this may be tough to find out and I know it sounds like it's straight out of a James Bond movie, but we need to know if any of the black SUVs the UN owns have what we call retractable licence plates. If they do then we can possibly link a UN vehicle, and possibly Goldberg, to the accidents." The suited man pauses and looks directly at Emily.

"Do you have access to the UN garage?" he asks.

Emily hesitates and looks at Hershel's face. The soft innocent kid she met at his home with his mother is now a face full of fear and paranoia. She takes a deep breath and informs the suited man that she does have access to the garage and can check the black SUVs here in New York. The suited man thanks her. The senior rabbi then looks at the suited man before turning to Emily and Hershel.

"There's more," the senior rabbi adds.

Emily strengthens her grip on Hershel's hand. The suited man informs Emily of other information that has come to light.

"Look, we have contacts, after all, the Jewish community here in New York…talks, you know? We know Goldberg is fully aware of the power and the ways of the Staff. His father met with rabbis here and in Israel. We have learned Goldberg has discovered his wife is having an affair."

Emily, covers her mouth again and shakes her head in disbelief. The suited man continues, this time looking at Hershel.

"As Goldberg knows what the Staff is capable of, he may attempt to look through the amber and perhaps even press it out of sheer frustration. You know what happens to people when the amber is pressed right?"

Emily, the novice, looks at Hershel and responds, "I read about that, I know what it does, but can the Staff really do that?"

Hershel nods his head and provides details to Emily as he looks at the suited man and the senior rabbi to expand further.

"It gets worse Em. You don't even need to look through the amber to know. If you press the amber all those around you are condemned in the afterlife. They are sent there immediately in an instant." Hershel is more serious than ever.

Emily is even more concerned,

"What do you mean they go there? They die? There and then?" she asks.

Hershel confirms with a hesitant nod.

The suited man persists. "We have come to the conclusion that Goldberg's anger has been triggered not just by all the events you mentioned but to add fuel to the fire he has discovered that either he is damned or someone close to him, perhaps his wife?" Emily is speechless. The suited man continues, more serious than before.

"We all know through the media about the in-fighting at the UN Council for Religious Coexistence and that it is not operating as successfully as the UN had hoped. We believe Goldberg wants control, he wants his pride and prominence restored and his instability right now may result in him resorting to desperate measures to let's say, 'correct' the issues at council."

Emily is in shock and stands, letting go of Hershel's hand. How did she not help to prevent Goldberg's demise? How did all this happen on her watch?

Emily informs the entire room that she is happy to help in any way. She volunteers to begin by checking on the existence of retractable licence plates on the UN's SUVs

The senior rabbi and suited man thank Emily for her honesty and ask her to give them time to consider a course of action regarding the Staff. She agrees and asks Hershel to accompany her out of the synagogue. Hershel doesn't stand.

"Wait a minute here. What if she gets caught snooping around? Are you guys okay to mess with a young woman's life and career?" Hershel protests pointing at the senior rabbi and suited man expecting an answer.

Emily walks over and holds Hershel's hand impressed with her protective boyfriend.

"Hey, I'm a big girl Hershel. I am in the UN garage every day, it's where I park. It's going to be okay," she reassures him.

As the pair walk out Hershel is concerned that Emily may be asked to do more in the future that will place her in danger. He thinks to himself that he should ask the suited man and the senior rabbi how he can help.

"Well there goes our Saturday," Emily smiles.

The couple walk out of the office and make their way out of the synagogue. Emily lets Hershel know she will call him in a few days once she has had a chance to confirm whether everything the suited man believes about the UN's SUVs is true or not. A cab pulls up at the front of the synagogue and she kisses Hershel. Emily glances at Hershel one last time as she closes the door and waves goodbye.

Hershel waves back and waits until the cab is out of sight before running back into the synagogue. He makes his way to the senior rabbi's office and enters without knocking. The rabbi and suited man are surprised by the sudden entrance which spurs the suited man to reach into his suit jacket as if reaching for a weapon. He removes his hand holding nothing. The rabbi raises his hand and motions for the suited man and Hershel to calm down, his other hand is lightly patting his heart. Hershel is a little out of breath.

"This whole thing is freaking me out rabbi," Hershel blurts out. "Whatever plan you two are going to devise, I want no part of it. I'm not afraid but I'm not trained in any of this stuff, I'm just a simple quiet student who had a grandfather with a story."

"Hershel, we know, and you feel like this because you promised your grandfather you would keep the Staff," the rabbi says to calm Hershel down.

Hershel feels tremendously irresponsible. Not only about breaking his promise but the events surrounding Goldberg, Rabbi Manassah, his flatmate and now Emily, and begins to realise that none of it would have happened if he was more accountable, reliable and mature.

"Rabbi, I should have just kept my promise. Look at me, I have $2 million and a beautiful girl. I should be the happiest man in the world but I'm a nervous wreck hiding in a synagogue." Hershel's voice gets louder with each word.

The rabbi again motions for calm. The suited man senses Hershel's state of mind especially his concern for Emily and decides Hershel needs a reality check.

"I understand how you feel about this Hershel but you must also understand, we are treading carefully with Emily. Do you really think she had no idea about the deaths of Rabbi Manassah and your flatmate? After all, wasn't it Emily that arranged the meeting between you and Goldberg? Do you think she just conveniently forgot to mention that you would be meeting with him and not just her at the café? You think she knows nothing about the Staff? She knew about the amber didn't she which means she must have had access to the information kept by Goldberg's father. She probably knows more about the Staff than you. It's time to grow up a little and see things beyond just the love in your eyes. Put that aside for a minute and look at the big picture. We are trying to help you and at the same time trying to prevent a significant world event if the Staff is misused."

The senior rabbi nods in agreement and briefs Hershel.

"If Emily finds out about the SUV plates then we know that Goldberg is somehow involved in what could be murder. Yes, we will ask the police to investigate any damage on the car or repairs that were made but only when we know more. It is important we keep you and Emily safe but remember our main focus is Goldberg. He has the Staff and we need to repossess it without him knowing."

Hershel sits back in his chair and begins to settle down. The suited man and senior rabbi look at each other before the senior rabbi offers a word of comfort and advice.

"Hershel, look at me. You have done enough here my son. There is no need for you to be involved with whatever plan the Shin Bet devise. You can stay here as long as you like but you also need to go to college and finish your studies. That's what Rabbi Manassah would have wanted no? The suited man will always be around to protect you. Right now, focus on what's important to you."

Hershel looks at the senior rabbi, he is right, he needs to get back on track. He needs to see his parents and go back to college. Some form of normality is desperately needed in his young life right now.

9

Desperation

For the Goldberg family, Saturday night has always been reserved for entertaining friends or UN representatives visiting New York. This Saturday night finds Isaac Goldberg sitting in his living room surrounded by nothing more than uncertainty. He sits in silent contemplation searching for solutions. Will his father recover? How can he transform the dysfunctional UN Council and why has his wife sought comfort in the arms of another man? He decides he must address these issues and take command of the downward spiral his life has taken before he hits rock bottom. Goldberg makes his way to the kitchen.

The ankle injury he sustained with the minor car accident has left him with a slight limp as he was too stubborn to go see a doctor. He takes comfort in using a cane but it's no ordinary cane. It is the Staff itself, which rarely leaves his side now.

As he enters the kitchen, he decides to confront his wife.

"Tell me, are you still in love with me?" he asks bravely.

"What kind of question is that?" his wife remarks, drink in hand and smiling as she turns to face her husband.

"You heard me, are you still in love with me?" Goldberg persists.

Mrs Goldberg's smile slowly disappears as she takes a sizeable mouthful to finish her glass of vodka. She is clearly intoxicated. Goldberg continues.

"I have noticed two sets of glasses and plates in the dishwasher on certain days. I'm not stupid, do you think I wouldn't know, in my own home?"

Mrs Goldberg is not in the least bit concerned and tries to justify her actions. "Isaac, you are never around and when you're here you're immersed in UN work or locked away in your study. It's turned you into a shadow. You live here but you are not really here. I don't know where you are. You just pop up from time to time and when you do, quite frankly, I get scared."

There is silence in the kitchen. Goldberg is speechless, his wife is right. She hasn't confessed to anything but she hasn't denied anything either.

Mrs Goldberg stares at her husband waiting for a response, then speaks emboldened by the alcohol.

"There is never a right time Isaac, I want a divorce. I know that won't come as a shock to you." She is done.

Goldberg has no response and shakes his head slightly in desperation. He is devastated and can't continue the discussion. He quietly leaves the room and walks to the study. Mrs Goldberg shrugs her shoulders and turns to face the other way. She goes back into her normal routine and pours herself another vodka.

It's early Monday morning and Emily leaves her brown-stone home to walk to her car. She sits behind the wheel and takes a deep breath. Today her investigation begins as she inspects the vehicles in the garage of the UN head-quarters. She looks around observing the city and the people. She listens to the sounds, the noise. Something seems different today. She's on edge.

As Emily arrives at the UN building the security measures required to get in and out of the garage make her nervous despite the fact she uses them every day. Emily scans her security pass and slowly enters the garage.

She makes her way slowly through each level and row before parking her car in her allocated bay next to Goldberg. She collects her things and gets out of her car. She looks straight up and notices the CCTV cameras located throughout the parking garage. They have always been there but today they feel like giant micro-scopes magnifying her every move.

Emily walks a short distance towards the elevators like she does every day. The UN's SUVs are always parked next to the elevators. Emily suddenly stops and walks to the front of one of the SUVs resting her back-pack on the bonnet and madly rummages through it. She accidentally on purpose drops a few items, some of which roll under the SUV. It's an acting display Meryl Streep would be proud of. If she is going to inspect the back of the UN's SUVs belonging to the security department, whatever she does will be outside her normal routine and quite noticeable on camera. Emily crouches down and looks under the SUV before standing and walking around to the rear. Unsure of whether she is out of sight of the cameras she moves quickly to check the licence plate on the SUV. Emily presses the licence plate inward hoping it would magically move but nothing happens. She pulls it towards her and tries pushing it up vertically into the car then down. Again, nothing happens. The plate won't budge and is secured by four screws. Emily picks up the roll of lipstick that made its way from the front of the SUV. She then moves onto the next black SUV and goes through her testing routine. Again, there are four screws securing the plate, it doesn't move. There is one more SUV.

Emily takes a deep breath and wipes the sweat from her brow. She makes her way to the back of the third SUV. She crouches down and pauses noticing the plate has no screws. She rubs her fingers along the numbers and it moves a little too much for an ordinary plate. She tries to push it in and activates a release mechanism. The plate retracts slowly upwards like a curtain and into the back door of the SUV. Emily gasps out loud before realising where she is and that she may be in view of the cameras. She tries to stop the plate from disappearing entirely into the vehicle by pulling it back down but it retracts fully. She leaves it alone. Emily picks up another roll of lipstick and stands, calmly making her way to the front of the SUV where she has left her backpack resting on the bonnet. She places two rolls of lipstick into the bag and places it on her shoulders before making her way to the elevators. She acts as if nothing has happened as the elevator doors close and she enters.

As Emily arrives on the correct floor she briskly walks to her desk and sits down before exhaling for 15 seconds. She is clearly flustered and tries to compose herself. She takes out her cosmetics bag and checks her make-up and dabs the beads of sweat from her forehead.

"Is that you Em?" Goldberg calls out from his office across the hall.

It startles Emily and she springs into action, notepad and pen in hand as she rushes on tip-toes into Goldberg's office.

"Yes, good morning. I thought I would come in early today. Lots to do," she says as she enters smiling pleasantly trying to look like she's in control.

Goldberg is sitting quietly and notices her nervousness and asks if everything is okay. Emily simply nods. Goldberg outlines his needs for the week.

"Em, as you know the council meets this week. It's our last meeting for a while thank god, so we are going to need the proposed agenda and last meeting's minutes sent out to members today. In the email to members we also need to ask them if they want to add anything to the agenda."

Goldberg stands from his desk to walk towards the window. Emily immediately notices he is using a cane.

"What's wrong with your leg?" she asks with her eyes firmly fixed on the cane. Goldberg turns around.

"Oh, the other night, the car jumped the curb and I caught my ankle under a pedal or something. It's just sore, a sprain maybe, it's not broken or anything. Does the cane make me look more distinguished?" Goldberg asks.

"I think it makes you look English?" Emily laughingly responds and Goldberg just smiles. It makes Emily realise that he hasn't laughed in some time. She looks at the cane and studies its features. She stares long enough to discover that standing right in front of her is the Staff. Emily wants to leave the office to hide her fear. She stays silent and looks away awkwardly, before looking straight at Goldberg who notices her unease as he turns away to look out the window. Emily eagerly breaks the silence.

"Um, I'll get started shall I? Just give me the morning to get the email and papers ready for you to review before I send them out."

"Thanks, Em," Goldberg replies still standing at his window staring at the view. Emily makes her way back to her desk and sits head in hands. The charade she has pulled off, pretending everything is alright, is hard work. She needs a coffee before she can even think about starting on the council papers.

It's Tuesday, three days before the last council meeting for the year, and Goldberg is sitting at his desk in his office at the UN building. He is busy reviewing the responses to Emily's email which provided the draft agenda for the last meeting and requested representatives to submit additional agenda items. Laying across Goldberg's desk is the Staff which he is admiring like a shining gold bar. There's a knock on the door.

"Come in," Goldberg responds and Mark Wells enters the room.

"Good morning Isaac, do you have a moment?" he asks seriously.

Goldberg gestures for Wells to take a seat. Wells takes a deep breath.

"Isaac, I have some information that you need to hear and make of it what you will." Wells pauses and notices the Staff on the desk before he continues. He has Goldberg's full attention.

"Isaac, one of our drivers noticed the rear licence plate on one of our SUVs had fully retracted. We never leave vehicles in the garage this way so we looked at garage CCTV footage just in case." Wells pulls out his cell phone and shows Goldberg a video of Emily disappearing behind the UN's SUVs.

"Is that Emily?" Goldberg asks surprised.

"Yes it is, and there's more," Wells responds concerned and disturbed by Emily's snooping.

"After I saw this footage, I checked on a few things. I came to your office that Friday you were away and she was in here. I checked with IT and someone logged in to your laptop with your password."

"Yes, she knows my password and besides I leave my laptop logged in. Maybe she was doing some work from my desk, she does that from time to time," Goldberg replies, watering down any concern before Wells continues.

"That's what she told me on the day but there is more. She also made a phone call from your office to Hershel Rosen and they arranged to meet."

Wells is more than concerned. He fears being caught and provides what he thinks is a "smoking gun" in the hope that Goldberg will order and condone some action, any action against Emily and perhaps even Hershel.

Goldberg is more than intrigued and stands with his cane. He walks towards the window, there is an uncomfortable silence before he responds, "Mark, do you think she knows? I mean, do you think she knows, everything?"

Wells' response is short.

"I think she knows enough. We need to at least confront her about the SUV."

Goldberg takes a deep breath and sighs before nodding his head.

That afternoon after work, Emily decides to drive to the synagogue rather than go home. She calls Hershel on the way and in a panic tells him an SUV plate retracted and that Goldberg is using the Staff as a cane. Hershel tells Emily he will inform the senior rabbi and suited man that she is on her way and that he will wait at the front of the synagogue for her. Emily agrees and cautiously continues driving toward the city.

Hershel paces on the steps of the synagogue under the watchful eye of the suited man and two security guards. Every shout, every loud noise and screeching of brakes and tyres, every siren and car horn forces Hershel to jump and look around. Emily leaves her car in the synagogue visitors' parking area and runs around the corner to the front doors and straight into Hershel's arms. They kiss quickly before the suited man ushers them inside.

The senior rabbi is standing outside his office and motions to the pair to come in and they sit at the desk. There are already glasses of water for them. Emily's hand is shaking slightly as she reaches forward to pick up a glass and take a sip. Hershel notices her nerves and places a hand on her shoulder. The suited man also notices she is nervous and speaks softly but impatiently.

"Emily, Hershel has briefed us a little, what exactly did you find?"

Emily takes another sip and places her glass on the desk. She begins to tell the men about her discovery yesterday in the UN garage and the existence of a retractable plate on the back of one of the black SUVs. The suited man takes a step back and looks at the senior rabbi.

"Well then it's murder," the suited man exclaims.

The senior rabbi's eyes roll into the back of his head.

"That escalated quickly." We are gathering evidence here and this is just another piece of the puzzle. A big piece yes, but there are many pieces before we finish. Very good work Emily." The rabbi smiles looking at the suited man.

Emily looks at the senior rabbi. "There's more. Goldberg has a bad ankle and uses the Staff as a cane. It never leaves his side."

The senior rabbi and suited man are silent and deflated. They contemplate the added difficulties this information brings; it certainly is a setback. The senior rabbi thanks Emily again and invites her to stay the night in the *shul*. She is scared and accepts without thinking twice.

"That would be good, thank you rabbi. Actually, I am a little hungry. Do you think Hershel and I could go across the road and have dinner?" Emily asks.

The senior rabbi approves and motions to the suited man to follow them.

The couple walk around the block to a nearby deli. Emily notices Hershel is quiet and decides that he is as nervous and scared as she is. Emily reaches over and holds Hershel's hand as they walk. He looks at her and provides a brief smile before looking straight ahead, the seriousness returning to his face.

As the couple enter the deli and find a table Emily notices the suited man remains outside.

"Aren't you going to come in?" she asks.

The suited man waves her away shaking his head. Hershel ignores the entire exchange and sits down burying his head in a menu. Emily senses there is something wrong as she picks up her menu.

She pauses to compose herself.

"What are you having?" she politely asks in the hope of easing the tension.

"I'm just having a Reuben sandwich," Hershel casually responds.

"Is that enough, doesn't sound like much of a dinner Hershel?" she asks caringly.

"I'm not that hungry." Hershel's reply is cold as he looks up for a waitress, making no eye contact with Emily and not waiting to see if she is ready to order.

The waitress arrives and takes the couple's order, two Reubens.

An uncomfortable silence falls around the couple. Frustrated, Emily strikes.

"Okay, what is it Hershel? If you're scared about all this so am I."

Hershel cannot contain himself any longer.

"Emily, I need to ask you a few questions and it's really important to me that you tell me the truth."

Hershel is a little angry and not the softly spoken man Emily has come to know.

"Okay, what do you want to know?" Emily frowns, she has nothing to hide and stares directly into his eyes.

"Firstly, when you contacted my mother to pass on Goldberg's condolences you already knew about the Staff didn't you?" Hershel pauses, he is serious.

Emily sits back, shrugs her shoulders and nods unsure where Hershel's line of questioning is leading. Hershel asks another question.

"Did you already know what the Staff could do and what it was capable of?" Hershel pushes the envelope in search of the truth.

"I had some idea of what it was, well a fairly good idea if the information Goldberg's father collected was right," she replies quickly and honestly.

Hershel rubs his hand across his mouth. He begins to realise this is all about the Staff and that he is merely a byproduct. These feelings Emily has for him might not even be real let alone a relationship, and the possibility of love is now the furthest thought in his mind. It's heartbreaking, and Hershel feels used and erupts angrily.

"If you knew all that then you also must have known about Goldberg's plan to kill Rabbi Manassah and my flatmate?" Hershel is interrogating an accomplice.

The food arrives at the table and Hershel looks up giving the waitress a fake smile. Emily continues to stare at Hershel and she defends herself with an attack of her own.

"Are you asking me if I knew? If I was part of my boss's murder plot?" Emily responds angrily.

Hershel shrugs his shoulders and throws his hands in the air.

"Well, with everything that's happening, I don't know what to believe anymore," Hershel says making no eye contact and waving a hand dismissing Emily.

As Hershel picks up his sandwich, Emily continues to attack.

"Listen to you, and you didn't 'pretend' to know anything about the Staff when your mother asked you what I was looking for?"

The waitress comes to the table to ask if the food is okay and whether the couple need anything else. Hershel and Emily are fuming as they stare at each other.

"Yes please, could I have this to take away? I'm just not that hungry right now," Hershel emphasises, as he stares at Emily as if she is the cause for his loss of appetite. He turns his eyes away and looks at the waitress who takes the plate away. Hershel stands and Emily drops her shoulders.

"Do you really want to do this now? They need us." Emily pleads.

Hershel smiles sarcastically.

"Actually, they need you. They need YOU now," Hershel says pointing to Emily making it clear that there is no us, no we. He stands staring at her for a moment raising his hands in the air waiting for a response but Emily can't provide one. Hershel starts to walk out. He arrives at the counter and pays the bill as the waitress hands him his takeaway.

The suited man notices Hershel walk out alone. He is unsure of what to do, follow Hershel back to the synagogue or stay behind at the deli and protect Emily, the only person they know at the UN and Shin Bet's best chance of accessing the Staff. He stays at the deli and Hershel realises he is right. It is Emily they need.

10

Goldberg's solution

It's Wednesday, the Friday council meeting draws near and Goldberg is sitting at his desk in his office at the UN building. Laying across his desk is the Staff which now seems to control him like a master would a slave. He is in deep thought about this final council meeting for the year. How can he leave the representatives of the member nations with a positive view of the council meetings and deliver hope and certainty for future meetings? Something like an act or achievement that shows he has made a positive impression that will eliminate any doubt that there is no one else as dedicated and effective for the position of under-secretary-general of the council.

Goldberg reclines in his chair and looks out the window at the view of the East River before looking back down at the Staff. His father's words echo throughout the room; *Do you know what one could do with its power?* A wry smile appears across Goldberg's face.

Goldberg looks at his phone before picking it up and calling his wife.

"Hello?" she answers.

"It's me *neshama*. Can I talk to you?" Goldberg's tone is soft and that of a beaten man. There is silence on the other end of the phone but he continues.

"Look, I know you want a divorce and I understand why and where I have failed you," he confesses but there is still no response.

"I need to ask you for one last favour. I'm pleading to you here. Look at what we have accomplished together and how much you have helped my career." This time his words are met with a soft cry and an almost inaudible sigh.

"I know you are listening; I know you would not want to see me fail."

Goldberg pauses before continuing.

"The favour I ask is to be with me at the UN. Attend the last UN Council meeting this Friday." Goldberg pauses again waiting for an answer, there is nothing.

"Look, I admit that it is a selfish request as the purpose of the favour is purely for publicity reasons and for my career," Goldberg reiterates.

Mrs Goldberg continues to listen. There is no real hatred in her husband's voice and she concedes.

"Okay Isaac, I'll do this one last thing, I'll play the happy wife for you," Mrs Goldberg agrees and hangs up immediately giving him no chance to respond.

It's early Thursday morning and Emily is having breakfast in the kitchen at the *shul*, alone. There is no sign of Hershel. Before long the suited man enters the kitchen and asks Emily to come to the senior rabbi's office when she is finished.

"I'll come with you now, I'm done," Emily responds as she finishes quickly. She looks up at the tea lady and says thank you for breakfast. She stands and follows the suited man to the office.

As she enters the office the senior rabbi asks her to sit down.

"Hello my dear, would you like a juice or another coffee?" he asks.

"No thanks rabbi, I just finished breakfast," Emily replies in a tired voice.

The senior rabbi smiles for only a moment. The suited man sits next to Emily. It's the first time he has sat down. Every other time in the office he has always stood to the right of the senior rabbi's desk. Emily instantly knows this is something important. The suited man begins.

"Emily, we are very grateful for the work you have done for us so far."

Emily nods in acknowledgement as the suited man continues.

"We need to ask you if you are prepared to undertake an even more important task for us?"

"You want me to get the Staff, right?" she says instantly and confidently.

The suited man looks at the senior rabbi and in turn both men look at Emily and nod dumbfounded. Emily is committed.

"Okay, I'm in, what's your plan, what do you want me to do?"

The suited man stands and paces around the room before he begins to slowly brief Emily as the senior rabbi pays close attention to the plan.

"Shin Bet operatives have been working on creating exact replicas of the Staff, clones if you want to call them that. Obviously, they don't contain any divine power but if you compared the clones to the real Staff one would not be able to tell the difference. We managed to build a few replicas from a combination of Rabbi Manassah's notes and pictures however there was information missing and although the replicas are good, they were not clones, not exactly the same in appearance. Then Hershel came along and it was his experience with the staff and facts like its size and weight that helped piece together the missing information we needed to make an identical Staff, a clone if you like. Talking about Hershel, where is he this morning?" the suited man asks.

Emily pauses before responding in a disappointed tone, "Well, clearly he slept in…let's just say what I thought was there really isn't."

The suited man is not perturbed, there are more important things than a lover's quarrel and he continues.

"The plan is for you to take the cloned Staff. Hide it in an umbrella cover we have specially made and insert it into the purpose-built umbrella pocket on the side of this backpack. You will transport the clone just the same as Hershel did when he owned the Staff."

The suited man then shows Emily the umbrella cover which has a built-in false umbrella handle to make it look like it actually contains an umbrella rather than just a stick. He then shows her the backpack with the side pocket which will securely hold the clone. Emily studies the equipment and it's perfect. She didn't expect anything less from Shin Bet.

The suited man pauses before adding, "I am sure you have already guessed what we have in mind. We need you to exchange, to switch the clone you will be carrying with the Staff. Do you understand?"

Emily puts down the umbrella cover and backpack and sighs.

"You do know that the Staff never leaves Mr Goldberg's side. I told you he uses it as a cane now. It is always with him at the UN building," she says.

The suited man knows the Shin Bet's best option for obtaining the Staff is for Emily to make the switch and he tells her to at least make an attempt. Emily understands and nods in acceptance.

The senior rabbi holds Emily's wrist.

"There is more my child," he says. "We know the UN Council meets this week. We also know that yesterday Goldberg has asked his wife to attend. We are concerned that all the 'troubles' Mr Goldberg is facing right now may very well push him over the edge. A man with so many problems and not many solutions may resort to acts of desperation, and with the Staff in hand who knows what he might do. Remember our teachings, it was Moses' frustration at the stubbornness of Pharaoh that resulted in the Staff summoning the plagues of Egypt. Do you understand? We are deeply concerned that the stubbornness of the UN Council and other frustrations may lead Mr Goldberg to use the Staff. You, me, us and the world is in danger of witnessing cataclysmic events unseen since the time of Moses," he concludes to Emily to ensure she understands the gravity of the situation.

Emily looks at the senior rabbi and the suited man and leans back into her chair upright and lifts her shoulders with pride.

"So, this means you want me to switch the Staff before the meeting, right? Got it. Let's check out these imitations you've built."

Emily stands and the men follow her out of the office looking at each other amazed at the ease by which Emily has accepted such a vital task.

The suited man opens the door to the locked room which holds the previous poor imitations and now holds the ultimate clone. He directs Emily past the replicas to a new cabinet where the clone lies like a holy relic in a bed of purple velvet.

"Hershel inspected all the imitations and none were good enough but when he saw and held the clone he said it was perfect," the suited man informs Emily as he takes a key and slowly opens the cabinet. "Hershel told us it is flawless and faultless based on what he remembers of the Staff."

Emily takes the clone not bothering to inspect it at all as she has never held the Staff itself. She places it into the false umbrella cover and attaches it to the backpack.

"Well then, I guess all our hopes are reliant on this bit of wood. Listen, I really have to get to work as I'll be late and don't want to raise any suspicions. I will try and make the switch at some stage before the meeting and let you know." Emily holds the senior rabbi's hand and smiles before turning to the suited man, who provides some last words.

"Remember our motto Emily, we are the 'Defenders that shall not be seen'." He reminds Emily of the importance of being covert.

Emily nods at the suited man before leaving the room.

The senior rabbi and suited man look at each other stunned. The bravery and calmness displayed by Emily makes her perfect for this assignment. The men leave the room and go their separate ways.

11

The assignment

The senior rabbi decides to pay Hershel a visit in his room at the *shul*.

Hershel has not slept a wink. He was falling in love with Emily only to realise he was simply being used to fulfil Goldberg's quest for the Staff. Before long there is a knock at the door.

"Who is it?" Hershel responds.

"It's me, your rabbi, who else?" the senior rabbi replies a little annoyed.

Hershel walks quickly to the door and opens it.

"I'm sorry rabbi I thought you were someone else," Hershel moans and flops back into bed. The senior rabbi walks into the room and closes the door.

"Sit up Hershel, this is important," he demands and Hershel obeys.

The senior rabbi sits down on the bed next to Hershel before delivering a sobering lecture.

"Look, I will probably be in the bad books of Shin Bet, Aman, Mossad, the KGB, FBI and maybe even the CIA for telling you this but you need to know."

The senior rabbi is serious and proceeds to tell Hershel every detail of the plan to obtain the Staff and that Emily has bravely accepted to make an attempt to switch the Staff with the clone at some stage before the UN Council meeting tomorrow. Hershel's face turns to one of concern. He clearly likes Emily and the senior rabbi senses it.

"Hershel, I don't know what happened between you two, but one day she adores you and the next day you're a schmuck. She is young but smart and more importantly, brave. Fix things with her." The senior rabbi ends his debrief to Hershel and taps Hershel on the knee as he stands.

"She needs someone like you Hershel."

The senior rabbi leaves the room. Hershel looks down, almost embarrassed at his actions.

As the senior rabbi closes the door behind him Hershel stands and begins to pace around the room muttering to himself, in two minds about what he should do. He quickly concludes that the rabbi is right and that he has acted like a bit of an ass. He has to redeem himself. His attention turns to Emily. He does love her even if she doesn't feel the same. How can he at least support her? He decides that Emily needs all the help she can get and begins to formulate a way to be inside the UN building on the day of the last meeting. He reaches for his cell phone and calls Emily's office number at the UN knowing she is on her way to the office and the call will likely go to a receptionist.

Goldberg is always in his office now, rarely leaving it other than to go home to sleep in his study. Even his meals consist of visits to restaurants, delis and cafes that surround the UN building grounds. He sits quietly at his desk contemplating his next move. The first step in his plan is already locked in as his wife has agreed to attend the last UN Council meeting for the year. Goldberg has decided that he has the perfect opportunity for revenge. Using the Staff, he will witness his wife's damnation into the afterlife.

Goldberg's corrupted mind has planned to go a step further. What if he pressed the amber while his wife was in the auditorium? He realises that using the power of the Staff during a council meeting will also deliver God's judgement to the UN representatives who deserve to be condemned.

Goldberg is pre-occupied with the thought but has not yet convinced himself that it's the right thing to do. He now spends hours doubting then convincing himself his actions are warranted. He justifies his thinking by looking at examples through history. The Israelites believed their use of the Ark of the Covenant in battle was justified as victory was essential; he too is in a position where success is essential as the world is at its religious crossroads. Goldberg believes summoning the Staff's divine power could possibly identify the one 'true' religion of the world as surely the amber would divinely select and condemn representatives who are followers of 'false' religions. What better place than during the last meeting of the year of the UN Council for Religious Coexistence to perform such an act. Goldberg edges a step closer to convincing himself that his plan is just.

As he turns his chair to look out his office window, he asks himself whether what he is doing would be construed as utilising a weapon of mass destruction, in this case a mass cleansing of sinners. He has no answer, preferring to ask himself a different question. If the Christians or Muslims or any other religion for that matter had possession of the Staff, would they use it if they were in Goldberg's position? In his mind the answer is clearly yes. Goldberg is satisfied. This is the solution. One true religion would surely put an end to all future religious conflicts. In addition, the act he will perform may go down in history as the Goldberg Protocol and potentially see him as a political legend in the annals of the UN. Furthermore, this will solve all his problems, even his father would approve and be proud of such actions.

Goldberg's joy is interrupted by the ringing of his phone. The UN main reception informs him that Hershel Rosen is on the phone returning his call. Goldberg stands and makes his way to his door and looks out at Emily's desk. She is not there and he slowly closes the door. He instructs the main reception to put the call through. He speaks first in a tone establishing he is several levels of importance and intelligence above Hershel.

"Young Mr Rosen, how are you? How are the studies coming along?" he asks superficially as he isn't remotely interested.

"They are going well sir, thank you. Actually, it's why I am calling. I know you have a meeting of the UN Council this week," Hershel responds shyly unable to hide his nerves before Goldberg interrupts.

"Yes, we do, an important one."

"Well sir, you see, I have this assignment, remember I'm studying political science? Anyway, it would be great to be able to sit in on the meeting, you know as a guest or visitor, if that would be possible?" Hershel asks nervously. He then remains silent hoping his acting is good enough to get an invite.

There is no response from Goldberg who is contemplating the request. He has become more than slightly paranoid since Wells told him about Emily and he knows she contacted Hershel. But Goldberg has become a powerful man, with the ability to wield an even more powerful weapon and nothing bothers him. He replies in a polite but disingenuous tone and succumbs to Hershel's request.

"Look Hershel, you helped me so it's the least I can do. I will leave your name at the main reception of the building, the access password for you is 'College'. Please make sure you don't bring any bags. Just bring photo ID like your student card, passport or driver's licence okay?"

Hershel says thank you and the men say their respective goodbyes.

Goldberg smiles. He is proud of his generosity, after all his plan has just been extended. He has ensnared another person that needs to be eliminated and now they too will be in the auditorium. It must be a sign. His plan is almost complete and Goldberg wallows in the success of his conjuring.

At around lunchtime Emily knocks on the office door.

"Come in," Goldberg instructs.

"Just wondering if you needed anything for lunch," she asks politely.

Goldberg simply shakes his head.

"You have everything for tomorrow's meeting, right?" she asks.

"I have everything and more Em, thank you," Goldberg replies smugly.

Emily frowns at the response and slowly moves back into the hallway.

A fierce morning storm blackens the New York sky. It's the day of the last UN Council meeting for the year.

Emily arrives at her usual time with her backpack complete with umbrella attached to the side pocket. She knows Goldberg is always in early and walks straight into his office to greet him. She takes a seat at his desk, a ritual on meeting days. She doesn't notice Wells in the room behind the door. Wells closes the door and Emily turns around startled.

"Oh, I'm so sorry, I shouldn't have just walked in like that," Emily offers.

It's a poor attempt at hiding her nerves and Wells knows it.

Goldberg tells her to forget about it. Emily leans down into her backpack and removes her notepad and immediately starts talking through the agenda for today's meeting and stops mid-sentence as she notices the Staff on Goldberg's desk. Her silent pause doesn't go unnoticed. She tries to continue but is interrupted as Wells walks towards the desk and sits next to her. Emily fidgets a little and takes a deep breath, clearly uncomfortable by Wells' presence. She hates Wells. Goldberg makes a point of re-introducing Wells to Emily to unsettle her further.

"We've met before, a few times, haven't we?" Wells adds.

Emily does nothing but nod. Goldberg begins softly.

"Em, my good friend here Mr Wells tells me you've been snooping around the garage. Is that right?" Goldberg asks innocently if coldly.

Emily knows she can't deny anything as Wells clearly has proof.

"Yes, well I was going through my bag and a few lipsticks rolled out. It kept rolling around, the garage is on a slope there you know. I couldn't find it and it's my favourite. I eventually found it behind one of the cars," Emily responds quickly and calmly in the hope of dismissing any suspicion.

"Mr Wells also tells me you called Hershel Rosen and met with him. Care to tell me why?" Goldberg's tone changes, he's a little angry now.

Emily plays it cool, pretending to get emotional with a gloomy façade.

"Yes, we met. I like him, at least I thought I did. I thought there was something between us but I assure you there's not," Emily sadly informs the two men.

Goldberg stands now, a little angrier.

"Emily, I thought more of you than a gold-digging whore. Tell me why did Hershel Rosen call me asking to come to today's meeting? Did you know about this?" Goldberg asks even more angry now.

Emily is surprised and Goldberg sees she is upset and clearly not pretending.

"I had no idea about that. Like I said Mr Goldberg, we met and there's nothing there, I assure you there's nothing between us," she pleads.

Goldberg nods his head and looks at Wells who acknowledges the gesture. Goldberg then sits back down placing a hand on the Staff on his desk.

"Em, thank you for telling the truth. I believe you. We have to finalise a few things before the meeting. Then Mr Wells will escort us to the auditorium."

"I understand Mr Goldberg," Emily replies.

There is a reason why Wells is hanging around she thinks to herself. Then it dawns on her, Wells knows. He knows about the power of the Staff. He knows that Goldberg will be pressing the amber today, he knows the plan. Emily is horrified. Even more tense now, she lowers her head and begins to go through her notepad at the list of required documents for the meeting. Goldberg looks at Wells and performs his trademark four-finger gesture across the top of his right ear. Wells nods, Emily must be eliminated. She continues to go through the meeting brief and looks up and notices Goldberg is not paying any attention or taking any notes.

"Sorry Emily, start again please," Goldberg smiles.

Emily goes back a page and starts again. She needs to make sure Goldberg has all the necessary papers in his possession. She finds it hard to concentrate as her mind is consumed by Wells' presence. The meeting will commence in little over an hour and she needs to somehow switch the Staff. It is beginning to feel impossible as with every passing minute the opportunity for Emily to switch the Staff narrows. The Staff does not leave Goldberg's side, ever, and to make matters worse, the Head of UN Security is sitting right beside her. Emily continues to go through the running sheet for the meeting all the while Wells stares at her. She can hear and feel his breath but she must stay calm. The pressure is unbearable.

After an hour of preparation Goldberg decides to leave for the meeting and head to the auditorium early. He stands, packs his small briefcase and begins to walk out of his office. Emily realises she has blown her chance. She picks up her backpack and follows Goldberg as usual. She needs to take the minutes.

As the three leave Goldberg's office and walk into the main hallway they are stopped by a UN security officer who is directing them to take a detour in the opposite direction as a small accident has forced them to clean the visitor's welcome area at the other end. The detour takes the trio past the rest rooms. Goldberg stops at the rest room door. He hands his small briefcase and cane to Emily and makes his way around the marble walled corner into the men's rest room.

Emily now has the Staff and briefcase in one hand and her backpack with umbrella cover in the other. It's impossible to make the switch and Wells is standing right next to her and uncomfortably close at that. The two are alone, there is no one else within sight or ear-shot in that part of the hallway. Wells looks around and realises he has an opportunity. He stares at Emily. She has never seen this look in his eyes before. She is scared. Wells notices Emily's hands are full and clearly defense-less. He turns and faces her and looks up and down her body. He gently reaches up to place his hand just below Emily's throat. She leans back to avoid the contact until a marble wall stops her retreat. There is no backing away. Wells smiles, a killer's smile. The smile they make when they realise they have full control over their victim. Wells then presses his body against Emily and keeps it there for an uncomfortable and inappropriate period of time. He slowly bows his head until his lips arrive at her neck. Emily can feel his breath, she can't move.

"You're so pretty," Wells whispers. "I want you but I don't trust you, I never have. I know you are up to something. Nothing gets passed me Emily."

Wells reinforces his physical and mental power over her.

Emily keeps her composure though inside she is petrified. She says and does nothing that would expose any sign of weakness. Wells turns his head and approaches the other side of her neck and again she feels his hot breath. This time his lips slightly and gently touch Emily's nape. He has gone far enough. Emily thinks quickly and realises her only defence are her legs. It's her only chance at getting away. If she kicks him and it isn't strong enough, he will retaliate and she dies. Emily summons the courage, takes a deep breath then swiftly with all her power raises her leg kneeing Wells hard in the groin.

As Wells bends over in pain, he looks up never losing eye contact with Emily on his way down and she stares right back at him. Wells kicks out a leg to make an adjustment in a move that he hopes will relieve some of his pain. As he does his leg accidentally presses the amber on the Staff. Emily watches as Wells' eyes roll back into his head, they turn white then close before he falls to the ground, unresponsive and lifeless.

At that moment a fire alarm sounds at the opposite end of the hallway. A man is quickly and suspiciously walking away. Two UN security officers run past Emily but stop when they see Wells on the ground.

"He fainted, passed out. I'll call first aid," Emily assures the men.

The security officers continue to chase the suspicious man who has disappeared near the elevators. Emily is finally alone and she hears a cubicle door slam open. She knows Goldberg will be out soon. Clearly, Goldberg was not close enough for the Staff to pass judgement on him. There is little time left to make a switch but there will be no other opportunity. It's now or never.

A few moments later Goldberg emerges and notices Wells on the floor.

"What happened," Goldberg asks but not too concerned.

"He fainted and passed out sir, I think he hit his head hard. I've called first aid," Emily replies calmly though she hasn't called anyone. She is now in control.

Goldberg collects his cane and briefcase from Emily all the while looking down at Wells.

"Mr Goldberg, you wanted to be early for the meeting, we'd better go."

Emily pushes forward and Goldberg agrees. The pair continue to make their way to the meeting. They come across two more security officers who raise a hand and ask the pair to stop. Emily is a bundle of nerves. What other obstacles will get in her way?

"Mr Goldberg, you need to know the alarm was faulty and there is no need for action. There are no issues from here and you are free to make your way to the auditorium," the security officers inform the pair.

After such drama the pair arrive at the auditorium for the meeting. Goldberg is standing tall and full of pride; he feels invincible as he mingles with the representatives of member nations. He briefly looks up and away to see if he can locate his wife in the auditorium. She is there standing in the corner of the visitors section but he thinks to himself she won't be leaving. Goldberg's thoughts turn to Hershel. He too will be present and what Hershel will witness will make sure he never contacts Goldberg again. He has given the order for Emily and with that Goldberg will have erased the last of his enemies that tie him to the Staff. He is more than prepared to make his move to impress the world.

Goldberg continues greeting representatives and begins asking them to take their seats. As they do he can already hear and see that the arguing has started. Goldberg cuts short his hand shaking activities and makes his way to his chair on the raised platform. He signals the deputy to call the meeting to order. The deputy begins and a representative shouts, "Can we at least agree on Gaza today?"

The auditorium erupts. Arguably The most religiously contested region in history is unexpectedly forced on the agenda and aggravates certain member nations. The deputy attempts to call the meeting to order and pleads with the representatives to adhere to the agenda. The meeting is an immediate disaster as per all the previous meetings. Emotion overtakes logic, strength of faith overturns composure and threats of military action overcome thoughts of peace. It is the worst meeting the council has ever had. It's a disaster and has not even officially commenced.

Goldberg listens and observes the ranting, raving, the challenges and insults flying across the room, not just from the representatives but also respected religious leaders. Goldberg looks down at the Staff hoping this would be the last time he and the world would have to endure such behaviour. He then looks across at his wife who is giving him the finger with a sarcastic, 'I really don't want to be here' smile. Goldberg's urge to press the amber grows. Should he press it now? The thought of pressing it right then and there consumes him. Yes, the power of the Staff is the best way forward for the world and for him. As the rambunctious meeting continues his anger grows. Goldberg and the world are keen to see an end to the hostility among representatives and member nations. He is engrossed in being the person who will instigate the identification of 'false' religions and leaders that will be deemed imposters by the Staff. All will be resolved as it will clearly identify what and who is right and therefore belongs in this world. There will be no more religious wars, and his purpose as under-secretary-general will be achieved making him a hero and resurrecting his UN career.

As the deputy's repeated calls for order fail Goldberg has had enough. Obsessed with the thought of possibly being recognised as the most powerful man in the world he finally brings the Staff up to his right eye. So pre-occupied with being seen as the conductor of good in this world, Goldberg hasn't given thought to whether he himself is damned. After all, he ordered the murder of at least two people but the thought doesn't cross his distorted mind. He is consumed with his strategy. It will correct everything.

Goldberg continues raising the Staff to his right eye. He wants to see who will appear on the other side. He wants to know, before any action, those who are con-demned. Emily has been watching Goldberg's every move. She has witnessed his egotistic, narcissistic anger-filled descent that has led to this moment. Goldberg's actions are interrupted by another explosive outburst between representatives. He lowers the Staff. Again, the deputy struggles to maintain order as Goldberg finally stands. He delivers a barrage to representatives.

"You, and you, you are damned," he screams pointing and warning.

The outburst is unprecedented by an under-secretary in the history of the UN. The auditorium quickly falls silent for a brief moment but quickly returns to its shambolic state as representatives talk over each other while the rest are fixated on Goldberg's behaviour.

Goldberg remains standing with Staff in hand and closes his eyes. He raises his left arm high above his head as if to indicate silence. He positions his right hand on the amber before he also raises his right arm high above his head. It's time. Goldberg pauses as the auditorium now falls silent as all eyes are on the under-secretary general. Goldberg wants to see the power he possesses and the outcome of his actions. He slowly opens his eyes and presses the amber and shouts, "God's will be done!" He then closes his eyes and tilts his head backwards as the Staff passes judgement to eliminate the damned. Silence falls around the auditorium. The eyes of every representative, journalist and distinguished guest are transfixed on Under-Secretary General Isaac Goldberg. Encouraged by the silence summoned by the Staff, Goldberg slowly brings his head forward and pauses to prepare himself for the sight before him. He gently and slowly opens his eyes.

Apart from silence, every person in the auditorium is still very much present and staring at him. Goldberg blinks to clear his vision, nothing has happened. He glances across at his wife who is clearly still alive as she again gives him the finger before she shakes her head and raises her hands in a 'what are you doing' gesture.

Goldberg stares blankly into the room and presses the amber again. He is confused and begins to sweat. He presses the amber again. His hair now uncannily out of place and with an increasingly disheveled appearance, Goldberg brings the Staff up to his right eye and looks through the amber and sees every representative clearly. He frantically presses the amber repeatedly. He is out of control. The council representatives begin to mumble to each other and all of them are focused on Goldberg's strange actions. The media present are recording every action on their cell phones eager to break this story. Emily slowly leaves the room and several disgruntled representatives follow, eager to contact their superiors and inform them of the incident.

The meeting is interrupted by the police who appear in every doorway of the auditorium, flanked by UN security officers. The posse of men make their way to Goldberg. They politely ask him to accompany them out of the room. Goldberg does not move. He is not the type of man to go quietly and demands to know the purpose for such an intrusion to UN protocol. Goldberg stands his ground looking down at the police who step up to the raised platform to arrest him. Goldberg pulls his arm away and again demands to know why.

The police inform him they have some questions regarding two hit and run incidents in the city. Goldberg stands cooperating with the police request and begins to walk quietly then breaks in a moment of weakness blurting out loudly.

"Remember this, you are all condemned," Goldberg yells. He is a beaten man.

How can his father have betrayed him with such a story? How did his successful career come to this? How was he seduced to the point where he thought himself worthy of exploiting the Staff's divine power? What led to his wife's betrayal? How could he have become so obsessed with the Staff that he ordered the elimination of people?

Goldberg is flanked by police who lead him to one of many patrol cars at the front steps of the UN building and usher him into the back seat. He sits motionless in handcuffs staring blankly into space as an officer closes the door. He is uncombed, untidy, unsettled, unruly and unimportant. Any respect and power he held at the UN is gone, not to mention his political career. Preoccupied and obsessed with playing God, he was oblivious to any thought regarding his own salvation.

Goldberg turns his head to look out the patrol car window. A large crowd has gathered at the foyer as people continue pouring out of the UN building. Goldberg tries to make sense of everything and amongst his blurred vision he notices Emily on the steps. She is carrying a backpack with an umbrella attached. The vision of Emily's backpack triggers Goldberg's memory. He instantly recalls Hershel transported the Staff in a similar fashion, umbrella cover and all when he brought the Staff to the café that day. Goldberg's stare turns to rage as he points at Emily and madly punches the patrol car window with his fist. Before long Goldberg stops. His antics go unnoticed. His shoulders slump as he collapses inwards. He begins to cry as he realises Emily has the Staff and that she too has betrayed him. He lifts his head and screams out loud. A scream bordering on madness. No one can hear him as his head jerks backward falling into the head rest. Emily doesn't notice him.

12

Aftermath

Emily continues walking away from the UN building towards the garage. The Police are everywhere and the crowds continue to leave the UN building spilling onto the surrounding grounds of the UN headquarters. Press from all over the world are eager to understand more of the story and look to interview any key UN executives who are willing to talk. They swarm the front doors and push against the steady flow of people leaving. Emily takes a deep breath and walks a little quicker towards the car park while at the same time trying not to look suspicious, smiling at fellow UN workers as she walks past. Emily gathers her thoughts and visualises the next steps she must take to get her task completed. Firstly, she needs to get to her car and drive home. She then needs to get a cab to the synagogue and finally she needs to hand over the Staff to the senior rabbi and the suited man.

Emily arrives at the security pad of the parking garage. She pauses for a moment to compose herself and looks back to make sure there is no one following her. She is alone. As she is about to insert her ID card into the security pad a man appears around the corner and places his hand on her shoulder.

"Excuse me miss," he asks in a deep voice which causes Emily to jump.

Emily slowly turns around, her heart pounding in her throat.

It's Hershel. Relieved, she falls into his arms and the two embrace.

"Oh my God you scared the hell out of me," Emily mumbles into Hershel's chest before she begins to cry, emotionally exhausted from the day's events.

"Emily, I'm so sorry for being such an arsehole," Hershel apologises as Emily begins to giggle wiping away tears.

"Hershel I'm sorry too…" Emily begins before Hershel interrupts.

"No, no, don't say anything. This was my responsibility from the start. I should have seen it through. I just left you to do my dirty work, please forgive…?"

"Um, we need to get to my car and get out of here first," Emily interrupts. The assignment is not over.

"You did it didn't you? Did you?" Hershel takes a step back not knowing.

Emily smiles and inserts her ID card into the security system. As the gate opens Emily grabs Hershel by the hand and the couple run to her car. Emily opens the door and removes her backpack with umbrella attached and throws it into the back seat where a *tallit* and pool cue case are waiting.

As they drive out it is evident the grounds and area surrounding the UN building are in lockdown. A police officer instructs Emily to stop her car. She obeys and rolls down her window. Before the officer can ask, she shows her UN ID to the increased police security at the gates. Hershel flashes his visitors card thinking he is important too. It's an anxious wait before the officer waves the couple through.

The couple stare straight ahead and drive a little further until they are a safe distance away and back on the streets of New York heading home.

"Hershel, what the hell were you thinking calling Goldberg and coming to the meeting?" Emily screams excitedly, shaking her head trying to be angry but ending up laughing.

"I had no intention of going to the meeting. I saw you with Goldberg and another guy then Goldberg went to the bathroom. I recognised the other guy with the security outfit from the café. He was bad news so I made a fire alarm go off down the hall," Hershel laughs.

"Are you kidding me, that's when I made the switch," Emily replies stunned.

"See, we are good together," Hershel says as he leans over and gives her a kiss on the cheek.

As the couple approach Emily's home there is already a cab waiting. They leave the car, grab the backpack and other items and jump into the cab instructing the driver to head for the synagogue. They are safe. Hershel and Emily kiss before Hershel pulls away to ask a question.

"You know, I really know nothing about you Emily and you have practically studied me. At least tell me where you're from?" Hershel asks as the cab driver takes a peek at the couple in his rear-vision mirror.

"Well now I can tell you everything, no more secrets okay?" Emily teasingly states to a relieved Hershel and begins to confess.

"Okay, I am from Israel originally, and my friends call me Em for short not Emily," she explains.

"I served with the Israeli military, national service, then moved to New York."

Emily is very matter of fact and Hershel is enjoying this side of her. Emily looks at him with a smile as they approach the city.

"Anything else you need to tell me," Hershel asks intrigued.

Emily looks into his eyes trustingly.

"Okay, the driver of this cab, he is Shin Bet," Emily says trusting Hershel now.

Hershel sits back and the cab driver greets him with a nod in the rear-view mirror.

"Oh, and the suited man at the synagogue he is my commanding officer." Hershel doesn't make the connection from the information and frowns.

"Yes, Hershel, I am Shin Bet too," Emily finishes.

Hershel pulls away clearly surprised and now a little frightened.

"Anything else Em, seriously?" He is stunned. Emily smiles apologetically.

"One more thing, I have a boyfriend," she sadly tells Hershel.

Hershel's jaw begins to drop as his face fills with disappointment. Emily leans across and her lips land on Hershel's open mouth. She kisses him hard then stops. Keeping her face inches from Hershel's lips, she whispers, "And he has two million dollars."

Hershel's disappointment quickly drains away as his face is filled with the elation only love can bring. He then kisses Emily hard.

The taxi drives through the city and is lost among the hundreds of yellow cabs on the streets of New York.

Present day in the Gaza Strip, the conflict over ownership of the territory continues unresolved.

Two young boys are playing, one a Jew the other a Palestinian, with the innocence of youth and carefree about their religious beliefs. They are following a bulldozer which is rearranging rubble. Sadly, given the quality of life, boys search through the ruins overturned by bulldozers as they look for items they can use or sell.

As the vehicle moves forward, one of the boys notices a black pipe and picks it up. He brushes it clean with his hand.

"Can I hold it too?" the other boy asks.

The two boys keep it and skip away together each holding one end of the black pipe.

It is the other half of the Staff of Moses.